CUPID'S BOW

When romantic novelist Janey first meets Ashe Corby, she is not impressed. But frustratingly, the hero in the latest novel she is writing persists in resembling him! As Janey gets to know Ashe, she comes to admire and like him. But when she attempts to help Ashe's son Daniel to realise his dream of studying horticulture, Ashe is furious at what he sees as interference on Janey's part. Miserable without each other, will love win through for them?

TONI ANDERS

◆

CUPID'S BOW

Complete and Unabridged

LINFORD
Leicester

First published in Great Britain

First Linford Edition
published 2013

A catalogue record for this book is available
from the British Library.

ISBN 978–1–4448–1790–4

Published by
F. A. Thorpe (Publishing)
Anstey, Leicestershire

Set by Words & Graphics Ltd.
Anstey, Leicestershire
Printed and bound in Great Britain by
T. J. International Ltd., Padstow, Cornwall

This book is printed on acid-free paper

Robin Hood

'Excuse me!' The voice was loud and authoritative. Janey quickened her footsteps. The forest path stretched ahead of her, lonely and deserted.

The voice came again.

'Miss Red Riding Hood, can't you read? There are plenty of signs. Put that dog on a lead!'

'Are you talking to me?'

'As you're the only person in a red coat and hood with a dog which seems to have a death wish — yes, I am!'

'Pixie, come here.'

The little Jack Russell peeped at her through a curtain of bracken at the side of the path, but stayed where she was.

'If she runs away from the path into the forest and you follow her, you'll both be in trouble,' the stranger said.

'I don't know what you're on about,' Janey said.

The man pointed to a sign on a tree.
FIELD ARCHERY. PLEASE KEEP TO THE PATHS.

'And there are signs over there and on the fence nearest to the road. I'm surprised you didn't see them.'

'I have my own way into the forest,' she said. 'I played here as a child. There was never any . . . ' she spat out the word ' . . . archery going on then.'

'Times change. The forest is under new ownership. You're allowed in, of course, but you must keep to the paths. They're marked with red arrows.'

'So that you can play Robin Hood and shoot poor defenceless rabbits and dogs?'

'We don't shoot animals, we shoot at targets.'

Janey looked around.

This had been a favourite playground in her childhood. She and Martin had spent happy days playing — well, yes, Robin Hood and Maid Marian. Now this modern Robin Hood was spoiling everything.

He came towards her, slowly but not threateningly. He was a little above average height, well-built, with a square face and a quiff of dark brown hair falling over one eye. She had to admit that he was very attractive.

He wore green, of course; a green coat and trousers and green boots. In one hand he carried a long flat bow.

'Where do you shoot?' She was interested despite herself.

He waved a hand.

'The butts are down there, about half a mile ahead.'

'Butts?'

'Targets. Would you like to see them?'

'No, thank you. I must be going. Pixie, come here.'

This time, the little dog obeyed her and Janey attached the lead to her collar. Then she pulled her hood over her head and fastened a button under her chin.

The man stepped back to the edge of the forest path and raised his bow in salute.

'The red arrows will show you the safe path back.'

Janey nodded to him and marched past, her head held high. She felt like a child who had been reprimanded. She longed to look back to see whether he had disappeared or whether he was watching her, but she kept straight on.

Pixie jumped around her, begging to be let off the lead.

'All right,' Janey relented, 'we'll go up to the common. You can run there.'

She pulled her hood further over her face. The spring breeze was cold. Little Red Riding Hood indeed! Despite herself, she began to smile. He *was* very attractive.

* * *

Ashe watched the small figure in the red coat walk away down the path. Not beautiful, he thought, but what an appealing face. Huge hazel eyes and thick, light brown hair. Nice. He'd like to see her again.

His long strides soon took him down to the clearing where a group of his friends were putting up backboards behind the targets.

My merry men, he thought, and grinned.

'What's funny?' Jeff asked. 'The sight of us working hard while you stroll around?'

'Someone just called me Robin Hood,' he explained. 'I decided you lot were the merry men.'

'We're not feeling merry,' Jeff said, 'we're worn out. Get your coat off and give a hand with these boards.'

Ashe slipped off his quiver of arrows and his coat and took the hammer Jeff held out.

'Who called you Robin Hood? A little old lady?'

'No, a cross young lady. Didn't approve of archery.'

'Well, let's hope she doesn't come here again,' Jim said.

'On the contrary, I hope she does come here again. I should like to know her better, perhaps convert her!'

* * *

Janey reached the car park and the path out of the forest and on to the road. A very large notice warned, *ARCHERY. THE PUBLIC ARE WARNED TO KEEP TO THE PATHS.*

She began to feel annoyed again. The forest had always been open to the public, not just to walk along certain paths but to go where they liked. Who was this Robin Hood to dictate what they could or couldn't do?

She led Pixie along the road to the Common. It was only ten minutes away. Soon the excited little dog was racing freely, returning to her for a pat before hurtling off again.

Janey sat down on an empty seat. What had he said? New ownership? She'd heard nothing about it! She'd ask Martin when he returned from France.

Her lifelong friend and employer had been gone three weeks, and she missed him. It was a responsibility to run the shop on her own. She'd be glad when he returned.

She glanced at her watch. Six o'clock. She stood up.

'Pixie,' she called. 'Pixie, come here.'

Pixie, investigating an empty polystyrene box, looked up, wondering whether to obey. Then, feeling the pangs of hunger, she decided to follow her mistress.

Janey always felt happy when she turned the bend in the country road and saw her little house ahead. Before she could open the gate, a car drew up beside her.

'Martin still away?' The driver was Dr Shepherd, an old friend of Martin's parents and now Janey's friend, too.

Janey picked up Pixie and Dr Shepherd stroked the little dog through the open window.

'You must be lonely.'

'He's been gone about three weeks, but he should be back next week. I'll be glad when he returns. The shop is a bit of a responsibility on my own.'

'I'm sure it's doing very well,' the

doctor said. 'Don't forget you can always come over and see Margaret and me one evening. Margaret loves to see you.'

'Thank you, Tom. Give Margaret my love.'

Pixie seemed to be waiting for her so she said farewell.

She put her key into the lock in the shiny black door. Pixie pushed past her and made for her water bowl.

'Good idea,' Janey said. 'I'll have a drink, too, before I do anything else.' She went into the little kitchen and filled the kettle.

The kitchen was at the back of the house and rather dark, so she'd painted it glowing yellow and filled it with orange crockery and utensils. The floor was covered with aquamarine-coloured tiles. The effect was bright, like Mediterranean sunshine.

Pixie licked drops of water from her whiskers.

'Now you want food, I suppose.' Janey reached for the little dog's dish. 'I suppose I'll have no peace until you're satisfied.' Janey filled the orange teapot, then lifted a tin of Pixie's favourite food from the cupboard.

While Pixie ate, Janey went into the sitting-room and put a light to the log fire she'd laid before leaving for work that morning. She watched as the crackling flames began to rise, then carefully placed a fireguard in front of it.

The cottage was tiny, just one room and the kitchen downstairs, and a large bedroom and bathroom upstairs. She had painted the walls a rich clotted cream, then filled each room with vibrant colours — ruby red, emerald green and sapphire blue. Rugs and cushions glowed and on the hearth, copper jugs reflected the dancing flames.

Janey went back into the kitchen and prepared a stir-fry, chopping the chicken and vegetables, enjoying the feeling of creating a tasty meal. She cooked for Martin once a week and in return he took her for a pub meal, or occasionally, if he'd made a good sale, to a restaurant.

She put her meal onto a tray and

carried it into the sitting-room, settling herself in an armchair near the fire. Pixie, tired out, dozed on the other side of the hearth.

Janey's mind kept returning to the encounter in the forest. Perhaps she should have accepted his invitation to see the — what did he call them? — butts. She'd met few attractive men since coming back to live in Burntwood three years ago.

She finished her meal and took her tray into the kitchen. Right now she had other things to think about. She went to her desk on the far side of the living-room. It had belonged to her father, one of the few things she'd brought from her family home when he died. It was long and had plenty of room for all the paraphernalia of her other occupation as a romantic novelist.

Her computer stood at one end and a small set of drawers for pencils, paper clips and pens sat at the other. In the centre were her notebooks and scribbling-pads. On the wall in front of the desk she'd nailed up a large pinboard. It was covered with notes to herself, plotlines and photographs torn from magazines, faces which would suggest her characters.

She sat down and opened a red folder. She'd begun to plot a new story last week and it wasn't going very well. The heroine was easy enough, she'd based her on Ceri, who was an actress.

The hero eluded her. She looked through the gallery of faces in front of her but none seemed quite right. She closed her eyes, seeking inspiration. He had to be tall and dark-haired. Suddenly she saw him with a quiff of hair which fell over one eye. The stranger in the forest! The archer!

No, she couldn't use him as a hero. He was arrogant, telling her what she couldn't do and where she couldn't go.

She opened her eyes. That wasn't true. He wasn't a bully. He hadn't threatened her. But she couldn't base her lovely hero on him. Or could she? Perhaps he'd start out as arrogant and the love of the heroine could change him.

What if she made him the villain? It was a Regency romance. He could have a black moustache and accost the heroine in the forest, she wearing a red cloak. He'd come galloping up, sweep her up on to his horse and . . .

She closed the folder and stood up. This was ridiculous. She'd do something else and return to her story later.

Pixie's eyes were slits, open just enough to watch Janey. If there was a chance of a game, she didn't want to miss it. Janey moved towards the kitchen and in a flash, the little dog was behind her, collecting a ball on the way.

'We're not going to play,' Janey said sternly, 'we're doing some gardening. I must plant those primulas I bought on Saturday before they dry out.'

She went into the garden. Still carrying her ball, Pixie followed. Janey collected the tray of primulas and a fork and made for the border at the edge of the lawn.

She put the tray of plants on the ground and looked around. Oh, for a strong man to dig and prune and weed, leaving her to do the nice jobs like planting the flowers.

I'm not a real gardener, she told herself, or I'd enjoy the difficult dirty jobs, too! She sighed again. She just wanted a pretty garden full of colour and scent.

Martin would give her a hand if he had some free time, but the shop took up all his days, and some evenings, too. And he was often away at sales.

Could she afford a gardener just once a week? She lowered herself onto the kneeler and began to dig a hole.

Half an hour later, she struggled to her feet, rubbing her aching back. She surveyed her work with satisfaction. The primulas, mauve, white, yellow and pink, made a colourful patchwork in the early evening light.

Pixie pushed the ball towards her hopefully.

'You don't give up, do you?' Janey

laughed. Relenting, she spent a few minutes throwing the ball across the lawn for the little dog to fetch.

'That's enough now,' she said. 'I must wash my hands. Martin might phone.'

They went indoors, Pixie curling up again near the hearth. Janey washed her hands, poured a glass of her favourite white wine and stretched out again in her chair. If Martin didn't phone soon, she'd do some work on her self-appointed homework. She was studying the history of costume jewellery with the idea of becoming Forge Antiques's expert on the subject.

Martin pretended to find her activities amusing, but she knew he was pleased with the way she'd quickly settled into her work at the shop. He relied on her more and more, and felt sufficiently confident of her abilities to take time off now and again.

Dear Martin. He was the son of old family friends, a few years older than her and who had always been in the background of her life. She'd spent holidays with his family as a child, but when he grew up and married she'd seen less of him. But he was always there.

His marriage had failed and he'd bought Forge Antiques in the village where he'd grown up. Janey had been keeping house for her widowed father and she and Martin had still seen little of each other. Then, when her father died, Martin had closed the shop for a few days and hurried to comfort her. She'd had no plans for her future, apart from a desire to write, and somehow found herself, a few weeks later, installed in the tiny cottage Martin owned in the village and helping him to run Forge Antiques.

That was three years ago. She and Martin were very close. But it was not a romance. Janey sometimes wondered idly whether she could ever be in love with him. He was not in love with her, she was certain of that.

She was twenty-two and had never had a serious boyfriend. That made her odd, she decided. She would like to have someone special of her own but, for the moment, Martin was the only man in her life.

Pixie was asleep and the ringing of the phone startled her into leaping off her cushion and on to Janey's lap.

'You sound happy,' Martin said once Janey picked up the receiver. 'You're obviously not missing me.'

'I am missing you,' she said. 'I'm beginning to be a little tired of being the boss of Forge Antiques. When are you coming home?'

'I should have thought you'd enjoy being in charge. How's business? Any luck with that Toby jug?'

'Yes. I put it in the centre of the window, and the very next day Mrs Potter from the garden centre came in and bought it. She said it reminded her of her husband. She's going to do a display around it.'

'That's the ugliest Toby jug we've ever had,' Martin said with a chuckle. 'Her poor husband!'

'You haven't told me when you're coming home.'

'On Thursday. Can you meet the four o'clock train?'

'Yes. Of course. I'll shut up early.'

'Janey.' Martin's voice was hesitant. 'I shall have a surprise for you on Thursday.'

'You managed to get those enamelled boxes?'

'No. Well, yes, I got the boxes, but that's not the surprise. I shan't say any more or it will spoil it.'

'OK, I'll wait. See you on Thursday afternoon.'

'I shan't ring again unless there's anything important. Look after yourself, Janey. See you on Thursday.'

He rang off and Janey sat looking at the telephone. He sounded as if he was holding something in. He'd gone to France specifically to buy some enamelled snuff-boxes, his particular interest. He'd decided to stay three weeks and travel around to various sales and antique fairs. But the boxes weren't the reason for his excitement.

She put Pixie back on her cushion and, going to the table, opened a large book on antiques. There was so much to learn if she was to be a real help to Martin.

She was trying to absorb a few facts every evening. She studied a page on the major porcelain factories. But after a few minutes, she gave up. It was no good, she couldn't concentrate.

What could Martin mean? Was he going to move to France? Unlikely, his French wasn't very good. Had he decided to sell the business? No, he'd bought some more enamelled boxes.

She slammed the book closed. It was no good. Her brain wasn't working properly. She looked at the clock. Eight-thirty. Too early for bed. She'd try her manuscript again. She moved over to the desk. Her computer stood waiting for the final draft of the story, but in the early stages, she preferred to use a pen and paper.

She picked up her pen. She must get

her hero sorted out.

Sir Willoughby de Grey dismounted and threw the reins to a hostler.

'Ceri, my dear, at last.' He strode towards her.

Ceri looked at the tall figure with the dark hair which fell in a quiff over his eye . . .

That wretched man! Janey threw down her pen. Now he had insinuated himself into her novel! He was determined to be the hero.

She picked up the pen again. Well, why not? The archer should be her hero. She knew nothing about him, so she could make him into any sort of man she chose. He would never know. She probably wouldn't meet him again.

'We Meet Again'

When Janey reached Forge Antiques the next day, she stood for a few minutes thoughtfully studying the window. Now that the large, colourful Toby jug had gone, she needed something eyecatching to put in its place. Of course, the very thing! She unlocked the door and went inside.

The interior was dark and shadowy. She moved around the shop, switching on lamps and creating pools of light. Then she went into the little office and quickly changed into a long pink- and white-striped dress. Martin thought it created a suitable old-fashioned ambience. Janey didn't mind; the dress was pretty and suited her.

She spent the next half-hour re-arranging the window. She placed the porcelain figures on one side: the group of children with a lamb, the Harlequin and Columbine and the Meissen rabbit. On the other side of the window she arranged a small collection of snuff-boxes and scent bottles.

But in the middle, in all its Victorian glory, stood a dolls'-house, its door left tantalisingly half-open revealing a well-furnished interior and little figures in each room. It was one of Janey's favourite objects in the whole shop. She would be sorry if it was sold. But it would be good to present Martin with evidence of her skill as a saleswoman.

She went outside to study her display and was well satisfied. Passers-by could not ignore her new centre-piece.

Back inside, she went around each object in the shop with a soft duster, then, donning gloves and an apron, polished a few silver knives and spoons which were beginning to show signs of tarnish.

The shop bell rang and she hastily removed the gloves. A small, plump woman came in, her eyes darting around the display as if looking for something.

Janey went forward with a helpful smile.

'Are you looking for anything special or do you just want to browse?'

'Don't frighten customers away by being too pushy,' Martin had warned her when she started work. 'Some people just like to look around before they admit they want a particular thing.'

But the little woman looked relieved.

'I want something for a young lady,' she said in an uncertain voice. 'It's her eighteenth birthday. My granddaughter. I wondered if you had any ideas.'

They wandered around the shop, Janey making suggestions which the woman considered and then rejected.

'Does she collect anything in particular?'

'She used to collect dolls but I don't know whether she does now. May I just wander around?' the woman asked. 'Something might strike me.'

'Of course.' Janey closed the lid and locked it and went to the other side of the shop to hang a picture.

'That's pretty.' The picture showed a smart art deco lady in a grey-green dress and a cloche hat. She carried a long, jewelled cigarette holder.

The woman continued to study the picture, then nodded.

'I'll take it.'

The shop door bell rang again. She turned round to see Ceri, her best friend, examining the dolls'-house from the shop side of the window.

'Very nice,' Ceri declared. 'A vast improvement on the Toby jug. Where is it, by the way?'

'Sold,' Janey said with satisfaction.

'I came at the right time,' her friend said. 'No biscuits, thank you. Must watch my figure. I've got a part in a film!'

'Ceri!' Janey squealed. 'How wonderful!'

Ceri made herself comfortable in a low Edwardian chair and took the coffee Janey handed her.

'Don't get too excited, I'm only a

lady of the court.'

'Lady of the court?'

'It's a mediaeval romance — you know, knights and ladies and so on. And Robin Hood, or someone like him.'

'Who's in it? Anyone famous?'

'No-one you'd have heard of. It's a small-budget thing. But English historical films are very popular abroad, especially in America, so you never know.'

'Where is it being filmed?'

'That's the funny thing. Here in Burntwood!'

'Here? But we haven't a castle or anything like that. Won't it be expensive to build sets?'

'Oh, no, not the castle bits. We're borrowing a castle in Wales for that. No, the forest bits are being filmed here.

Ceri glanced at her watch.

'Goodness, is that the time? I must fly. Rehearsal this afternoon.' She put her coffee mug on a shelf and stood up. 'I really only popped in to give you an invitation.'

'Invitation?'

'Yes. To a party. This evening.'

'Rather short notice.'

'Well, you know what theatricals are like. Impulsive.'

Janey didn't know, but nodded.

'Any time is party time,' Ceri went on gaily. 'I've been invited and I can bring a friend. You need a bit of cheering up when you've been without your Martin for so long.'

'He's not my Martin!' Janey protested. 'But I agree a party might be fun. Where is it?'

'Not far away. Someone in the company has a house on the far side of the forest. I have the directions somewhere. I'll pick you up at eight. OK?'

When she'd gone, Janey wandered around the shop, rearranging a group of old toys, straightening a picture. She was excited at the thought of a party but a little apprehensive at the prospect of an evening with strangers.

What should she wear? She wished she had consulted Ceri. Was it to be jeans and T-shirt, or a very stylish affair?

The bell on the door tinkled again. Janey was surprised to see a young man of about fifteen standing just inside the door and looking nervously around. Antiques shops seldom attracted teenagers.

She smiled and pretended to be busy at a bookshelf but watched as he began to prowl around the shop. He had an open face and large, awkward hands.

He picked up and examined a few ornaments, replacing each carefully on the table.

'Are you looking for a present for someone?'

'Girlfriend,' he muttered.

Janey was surprised. Surely young girls of his age preferred CDs or perfume to antiques.

'She collects rabbits.'

'Rabbits?'

'Rabbit ornaments. China and wood and so on.'

Janey left the books and joined him at the table of small animals. In the middle was a little silver rabbit sitting up on its back legs with its front paws in the air.

'How much?' the boy asked.

'Fifteen pounds,' Janey replied. 'Is that too much?'

The boy nodded and began to look around again.

The shrill ringing of the telephone startled them both. Janey went to the corner of the shop where the telephone stood. As she picked it up, she looked across to the mirror which was facing the boy. His hand had snaked out towards the silver rabbit and in a second it was in his pocket.

'Just a thought,' Ceri's voice said in her ear. 'I wanted to warn you we'd need to be dressed up tonight.'

'I thought we might be. Thanks.'

She slowly replaced the telephone and looked at the boy. He gazed back at her without flinching.

What should she do? Slowly she walked past him to the shop door, bolted it and stood with her back against it. He was young but bigger than her. She took a deep breath.

'Will you put the rabbit back on the table.'

It was a command, not a question.

He looked at her but said nothing.

'I shan't unbolt the door until you do.' She breathed deeply to control her legs which threatened to shake. 'I'm sure you don't want me to call the police.'

Slowly he reached into his pocket and pulled out the little rabbit. Then he put it carefully back on the table.

Janey breathed out.

For a few minutes they stood looking at each other. Then, surprising herself, Janey said, 'Would you like a cup of coffee? I was just going to make one.'

He looked at her in surprise, then nodded.

'Thanks.' He had a pleasant voice and obviously wasn't a young thug, Janey decided with relief.

Janey found some chocolate biscuits and watched him tuck in.

'What's your name?'

'Daniel.'

'Daniel what?'

'If I tell you, you'll know who I am. Daniel will do. And I shan't give you my address.'

'Are you still at school?'

He nodded, his mouth too full of biscuit to reply.

'What do you want to do when you leave school?'

He swallowed some coffee before replying.

'What I want to do and what my father will make me do are two different things.'

It was the most he had said since entering the shop. He spoke with passion, as though the thought had been bubbling away inside him for some time.

Janey waited.

'Would it help to talk? Perhaps it would be easier than talking to your father or your mother.'

'I haven't got a mother. She died when I was born. There's only Father

29

and me.' He looked down at his hands, then seemed to make up his mind.

'Father loves the family firm and thinks that when I'm ready to work, I'll want to join him. But I won't. I want to do something quite different.'

'You want to paint?' Janey guessed.

'No. I want to design gardens. I love gardening. I want to go to horticultural college. He won't hear of it.'

Janey looked at the mutinous young face in front of her.

'Look, this is just a suggestion, but what if you did something to show him that you're really interested in gardening? That might influence him.'

'Like what?'

'I have a garden at my cottage. It's not very big but it's more than I can handle. I need someone to give me a hand — dig the borders and cut hedges and so on. If you were interested you could come for a few hours a week. We could take photos to show what you're doing and then some of the finished results when you'd grown things. I'd pay you, of course,' she added.

Daniel considered.

'I could come for a few hours after school. I wonder if it would work.' Then his face fell. 'What about . . . ?' He looked towards the shop. He was obviously thinking of the incident with the silver rabbit.

'I'm sure nothing like that will happen again.' Janey stood up and collected the coffee mugs. 'But you must realise that, if it did, I should have to inform the police.'

'It won't,' he said seriously. 'It was a . . . a lapse. I'm not like that. It's just that I wanted to give Carli a rabbit and I don't get much pocket money.'

'Well, now you can earn some!' Janey smiled. 'Would you like me to put the rabbit on one side until you've earned enough to pay for it?'

'I would. And I'll work hard. I'm very strong.'

'I can see you are,' she said solemnly. 'I shouldn't have offered you the job otherwise.'

It was a very different boy who left the shop ten minutes later, promising to turn up the following afternoon.

'I hope I won't regret it,' Janey muttered as she bolted the door again, turned the sign to *CLOSED* and made her way upstairs to Martin's flat.

Pixie, asleep on a cushion, stretched and yawned.

'Come on, lazybones.'

Pixie yawned again and, jumping off the chair, licked Janey's hand in greeting.

She fed the little dog and made herself a cup of tea and unpacked a sandwich. There was no housework to be done. She'd given the place a good clean when Martin left. It would only need a dust the day before he came back and perhaps a vase of fresh flowers. She decided to make a lemon cake to welcome him home. She switched on the radio and hummed quietly to herself as she worked.

Soon the flat was full of the sweet scent of lemon. She popped the cake into the oven and sat down with her feet on a little stool, waiting for it to cook.

She thought again of the young boy, Daniel. She wondered where he lived. She had never seen him before. Would he turn up tomorrow? He seemed very keen.

Her mind drifted to what to wear to the party. Would there be time to wash her hair?

The timer pinged and she slid the cake out of the oven. It was perfect, risen and golden and ready for icing. She placed it on a rack to cool.

At four, Janey decided to close the shop and go home. She removed the long dress and put on a pair of jeans and a T-shirt. Then she slipped upstairs, put the cake into a tin and collected Pixie.

'Come on. Time to go home.'

Pixie's ears pricked up and she stood obediently while her lead was fastened. Janey seldom took her car to work. Pixie needed a walk and the cottage was only half an hour away. They left the shop.

'Janey, hi! Haven't seen you for a while. How are you?'

Janey's heart sank. Kevin Shaw-Coles, Martin's best friend. Janey disliked him intensely for no reason that she could explain.

'Hello, Kevin. I'm fine, thanks.'

'When's Martin coming back?'

'On Thursday. I'm sorry, Kevin, I must go. I've a party invitation for tonight and I need to get ready.'

'I could run you home. The car's just round the corner.'

'It's very kind but no, thank you. Pixie needs a walk. She's been in the flat all day.'

'I'll walk with you, then. I need to stretch my legs. Been sitting in the office for hours.'

They walked in silence for a few minutes. They turned a corner into the lane which led to Pippin Cottage. Kevin took her arm.

'Will you let me take you to dinner tomorrow evening?'

Janey had had a feeling that some

such invitation was coming. On the pretence of tightening Pixie's collar, she removed her arm from his hand.

'I'm sorry,' she said, as she stood up, 'I shall be busy tomorrow. Martin will be home the next day and I must make sure everything is ready.'

'Martin won't mind if a few things are out of place.'

'But I will,' she said firmly. 'Thank you for the invitation, Kevin, but perhaps some other time.'

They reached the cottage and she stepped inside the gate.

'Quick cup of coffee?'

'I'm sorry. I told you, I'm going out. Thank you for your company, Kevin. Bye.'

She opened the door and went inside, locking it firmly.

'That man!' she muttered. 'That wretched man.'

Martin could never understand why she always refused Kevin's invitations.

'He's quite good-looking, and well-off with a nice house by the river. Why don't you like him?'

Janey had just shrugged and muttered something about him not being her type. She couldn't explain. There was just something about him . . .

She peeped out from behind the curtain and breathed a sigh of relief when she saw that he had gone.

★ ★ ★

Ceri arrived at eight, dressed to be noticed. She wore a black, flapper-style dress, with layers of silky fringing down the skirt and very high heels. Janey wondered whether her own outfit looked dull in comparison. But Ceri's first remark reassured her.

'Wow! I love your dress.'

Janey's dress fell to her ankles in an abstract pattern of pale pink and deep plum. The skirt was full and swirled around her as she walked. Her only ornament was a wide silver bangle.

Pixie, sensing that an outing might be possible, jumped about excitedly. Janey gave her a small chocolate treat.

'No,' she said gently, 'you stay here. I shan't be long.'

Pixie crept into her basket and gazed reproachfully over the side at the two girls.

Ceri's car was an ancient 2CV, her pride and joy. Janey looked at it doubtfully.

'Will it get us there?'

'Would you rather walk? Get in and be grateful!' Ceri switched on the engine and the car pulled away.

They bowled along past the forest.

'I met a really dishy man in there.' Janey waved a hand towards the trees. 'I was taking Pixie for a walk and he told me off for not sticking to the paths. Bit of a cheek, I thought, but he was very attractive.'

'What was his name?'

'I've no idea. We didn't really chat.'

'What a waste. There aren't so many dishy men in this place that you can let one get away.'

'Who's giving this party?' Janey asked after a while.

'A friend of the director, Wynn. He thought it would be a good idea for everyone to meet and have a fun evening together before the real work of filming began. Hey, I wonder if that's the house?' She stopped the car and consulted her instructions. 'It's called Forest Mere.'

'Yes. There on the wall.' Janey pointed to a sign.

Ceri turned into a very short lane at the end of which was a large, sprawling country house. The drive was full of cars and people were strolling about.

Janey got out of the car and gazed about her. The forest came right to the edge of the garden and, on the other side, fields stretched as far as the eye could see.

As they neared the house they could see a large table where a group of people sat as if waiting for guests.

'There's Wynn in the middle,' Ceri told her. 'I recognise the woman with red hair. She's wardrobe. And I think the blonde is Wynn's secretary. I don't know anyone else. I've never seen that striking-looking man at the end.'

But Janey had. Her steps slowed as she approached the table. It couldn't be. But it was. Robin Hood.

'Well, Red Riding Hood. We meet again,' he said.

At The Party

Ceri spotted a friend and left Janey's side. Janey stood face to face with Robin Hood. He was smiling at her in an infuriating way.

'Why didn't I guess it might be your house?' she asked. 'Do you own the forest, too?'

'As a matter of fact . . . '

'I might have known.'

'Don't hold it against me,' he said, taking her arm. 'Come and have a drink to cool you down. You're not in the film, are you?' he asked when they both had a drink.

'No, I came with a friend. I'm not in it. Are you?'

'No, I'm no actor. Wynn, the director, is an old friend. My house is suitable for a large party so we had it here.'

Janey looked around.

'The garden is beautiful. Is it all yours?'

'Yes. And the fields beyond. It's quite an estate.'

'Plus the forest,' Janey reminded him. She sipped her fruit cup. It was delicious.

'Do you live here in the village?'

'Yes. In Pippin Lane. I have Pippin Cottage at the beginning of the lane.'

'Oh, the dinky little black and white house?'

'I suppose. Compared with this, it is dinky.'

'Compared with anything.' He laughed. She joined in the laughter.

'I suppose it isn't, but it's mine and I'm very fond of it.'

'Would you like to see Forest Mere, or would that be rubbing it in?'

Janey placed her empty glass on a table nearby.

'I'd love to see it. Other people's houses fascinate me.'

The front door was standing open. They stepped into a cool wood-panelled hall with a flight of polished stairs leading off to the right.

He threw open a door on the left. Janey gazed around the wide room with its windows sweeping across one wall.

'What a beautiful room,' she said, 'and what a lovely view.' She went to the window and looked out across the garden and the fields beyond to the edge of the forest.

'It is beautiful, isn't it?' he said, coming to stand behind her. She was conscious of his nearness and the soft, powdery scent of his aftershave.

'How long have you lived here?'

'Six months. I inherited it when my uncle died.'

'Your uncle was Sir Rex Corby?'

He bowed.

'Ashe Corby, at your service.'

'Well, at least I know your name now. Robin Hood was a bit outlandish.'

'And what do I swap for Red Riding Hood?'

'Janey Robbins.' They shook hands solemnly.

'Let me show you some of the other rooms.'

They went through another reception room decorated entirely in cream except for a pile of blue cushions on the cream couch.

'This is restful,' she commented.

Upstairs, the bedrooms were luxuriously furnished, each with a different predominating colour. From the bedroom windows she could see the guests wandering about the gardens. She caught a glimpse of Ceri's flirty black dress. There was no-one else upstairs.

'I think we should join the others,' she said a little nervously.

Ashe agreed readily and led the way to the stairs.

'Time for another drink,' he said.

Outside, they strolled through a formal garden whose flower-beds were edged with tiny box hedges.

'My uncle was influenced by Elizabethan knot gardens, I think.'

'I think they're very pretty.'

Janey turned to look back at the

house. The walls were white and softened by luxuriant deep green creeper. To the right of the house and through some trees the soft blue of a lake shimmered in the evening light.

'May I go and look at it?' she asked. 'I love lakes.'

'I'll take you.' He put a hand under her arm.

'I mustn't take you away from your guests.'

'They're not strictly my guests. It's Wynn's party.'

The lake was small but perfect. It had a flotilla of ducks and moorhens in the bullrushes at the far end.

'Do you swim in it?'

'No. We have a heated pool behind the house.' Ashe glanced at his watch. 'Time for supper.'

Supper was laid on tables in the huge kitchen, every surface covered with plates of meat, savouries, cheeses, fish and fruit.

'I'm afraid I must leave you for a while. Please help yourself. I have to speak to Wynn.'

As soon as he'd left, Ceri joined Janey.

'You're a dark horse,' she said. 'I didn't know you were such a friend of our host.'

'It's him! Robin Hood from the forest.'

Ceri was busy filling her plate.

'I daren't have sausage rolls or trifles,' she said, unhappily. 'This dress is so tight it will pop.'

'Did you hear what I said? He's my dishy man!'

Ceri took a glass of wine.

'I heard you. But remember this is a party. Tomorrow will be different. Don't go overboard for him.'

'I shan't.' Janey began to make a selection of food. 'You were the one who talked of playing my cards right.'

'That was a joke. I don't want you to get hurt.'

They carried their plates to a bench by the lawn.

'Just smell the air.' Janey breathed

deeply. 'I've discovered his name.'

'Whose name?'

'Robin Hood's, of course.'

Ceri wiped her fingers on a napkin. 'Tell me.'

'Ashe Corby. Mean anything?'

'No. Perhaps he's just a friend of the director.' She stood up. 'I'm going to get a refill for this.'

'Should you? You're driving.'

'It's non-alcoholic, Grandma,' Ceri replied rudely.

When they returned to the house they found a small group of musicians tuning up ready for dancing.

'Janey. Fancy seeing you here.' Janey turned and found Dr Shepherd smiling at her.

'I might say the same thing,' she replied.

'I'm a friend of Ashe Corby and he asked me along. Margaret couldn't come. Are you a friend of his, too?'

'No, I came with a girl who's in the film.'

'May I have the pleasure?' They

joined the couples circling the floor.

'Actually I have met Ashe before — once,' Janey said. 'He was playing with a bow and arrows in the forest.'

'Playing!' Dr. Shepherd gave a laugh. 'He's a very fine archer. And a fencing master, too.'

Janey looked impressed.

'That explains a few things.'

'Perhaps he's giving advice on the film.'

Dr Shepherd tried a bit of fancy footwork and Janey was pleased when she could follow him.

'Tell me more about Ashe Corby.'

'He's a clever man and very hard-working. His elder brother inherited the family firm, but turned to drink and nearly lost the business. Ashe took it over and made it into a very successful undertaking.'

The music ended.

'I'd better be going.'

'Give my love to Margaret.'

She wandered into the kitchen. Ceri was there, eating a dish of ice-cream with a guilty expression on her face.

'What about the tight dress?'

'Couldn't resist ice-cream. Want some?'

'I do,' a voice came from the doorway.

Janey made the introductions. Then she took a tub of ice-cream from the freezer, filled two dishes and gave one to Ashe.

'Come on, let's go and eat it in the garden,' he said.

Just then a young man stuck his head round the door.

'Come on, Ceri, you promised me a dance!'

Ceri gave her friend a grin and slipped out.

Janey followed Ashe.

'What is your connection with the film?' she asked when they'd finished their ice-creams. 'Dr Shepherd said you fence as well as shoot. But you're not in the film.'

Ashe took a deep breath.

'Wynn asked me if I could act as

advisor for the fight scenes and also train the actors. I agreed.'

'How interesting!'

He nodded.

'Now tell me something about yourself. Do you live alone in Pippin Cottage?'

'No. There's Pixie.'

'You know what I mean.' He smiled at her. 'I'm trying to discover whether there's a special person in your life.'

'Yes,' she said simply, 'my boss, Martin. He has a flat above the antiques shop, and he looks out for me. There's nothing romantic between us,' she admitted, 'but there might be one day.'

He frowned.

'It sounds like a strange relationship.'

'When my father died — I kept house for him — I had no one. So Martin suggested I come to Burntwood to help him run his antique shop until I decided what I wanted to do. He owned Pippin Cottage. It was empty so we decorated it and Pixie and I moved in.'

'Are you in love with him?' Ashe asked bluntly.

'I feel grateful to him, I like him a lot. I know he goes out with other girls but he seems to like having me around.'

'He's a very lucky man.' Ashe picked up their dishes. 'Come on, let's dance. Do you like dancing?'

'Oh, yes. Not that I get much opportunity.'

In the kitchen, a young man was filling the dishwasher.

'Daniel!' Janey and Ashe said together. Ashe looked at her.

'You know my son?'

His son! Janey looked from one to the other. Yes, there was a resemblance.

'We met at the shop,' Janey said. 'Daniel came to look round one day.'

'I didn't know he was interested in antiques.'

'You don't know what I'm interested in,' Daniel replied sulkily.

'Daniel offered to see to the washing-up for a small payment,' Ashe told her wryly.

'Nothing wrong with that. I had a

Saturday job in a shop when I was his age.'

Daniel threw her a grateful glance.

'Come on,' Ashe said. 'Let's dance.'

As they danced, Janey thought of the young man in the kitchen. So he was Ashe Corby's son. What would Ashe say if he knew she'd offered Daniel a job working in her garden? She had a feeling he might not be pleased. But she couldn't go back on her word to Daniel.

'Penny for them,' Ashe said.

'They weren't worth a penny.' She laughed.

'I can't understand why we've never met before.'

'The village isn't very big,' Janey mused, 'but I'm mostly at home or in the shop.'

'The antiques shop?'

'Yes. Forge Antiques. Perhaps you don't go into antiques shops.

'Not often,' he agreed. 'Of course, if I'd known you'd be there, I'd have called in long ago.'

51

He pulled her closer to him. He was a great deal taller than her but they fitted together perfectly. Together they twirled and glided around the room. Clasped firmly in his arms, Janey gave herself up to movement and the music.

'When do you start your work on the film?'

'Not for a few weeks.'

'Your business is in London?'

'Yes. I have a tiny flat up there and I often stay over.'

The music came to an end.

'Let me get you a drink.'

Janey sank on to the nearest chair, glad of the rest.

'Here she is!' Ceri slid into the seat next to her. 'Let me introduce you to Kyle Grey.'

She indicated a handsome young man with fair curls.

'He's the star of the film.'

Kyle rather affectedly kissed her hand. Getting into the part already, Janey decided.

The music started again and the

young couple went off as Ashe returned with two glasses.

'Would you let me . . . ' He started when the grandfather clock in the hall began to chime and drowned his words.

'Midnight,' Janey said. 'I think we should be leaving.'

'So you're Cinderella now?' He laid a hand on her arm. 'Would you let me take you to dinner one night?'

'Well, I . . . '

'Please. I'll ring you to arrange it.'

'OK, thank you. But Martin will be back from Paris in a couple of days. I don't want to make plans in case . . . '

'In case he wants you.' Ashe was short. 'I understand. I'll leave it — if you'll promise to come.' He gazed at her intently.

Janey felt her stomach lurch. Did this man really want to take her out? Surely he had plenty of lady friends.

As if he could read her thoughts he took both her hands in his and gave her a quick kiss on the forehead.

'I've really enjoyed this evening. I hope you have.'

Before she could reply Ceri appeared again, but without Kyle Grey. Her face was flushed and shiny.

'It's been a wonderful party,' she said to Ashe, 'but I'm afraid we must go now. Work starts in earnest tomorrow.'

As they drove away from Forest Mere, Janey looked back. Ashe was standing, arms down at his side, watching them.

★　★　★

Daniel was on holiday the next day so he arrived early, anxious to begin work. While Janey made him a packed lunch, he had a quick game on the lawn with Pixie.

Janey was pleased. Pixie would be tired and prepared to sleep at the shop.

She was engrossed in her task and failed to notice the boy come into the kitchen doorway and lean against the door jamb, watching her.

'It's kind of you to make those for me,' he said. 'I could manage till I get home.'

'I don't want you to feel too weak to work,' she said with a laugh. 'Orange juice or apple?' She held up two bottles.

'Apple, please.'

Janey took a small freezer box from the pantry, added ice packs and placed the sandwiches and apple juice inside.

'There. Put the box in the shed and it will be ready when you want it.'

He took a mobile phone from his pocket.

'I'll phone Carli and say I won't be there for lunch.'

'Carli?'

'Our housekeeper, Mrs Carlson. She brought me up. She fusses over me, but she loves me . . . and I love her.' He coloured a little but said this simply.

Janey gave him a warm smile, glad that he had someone like Carli in his life.

'When my father said I was helping for the money, it wasn't just that. Carli had been busy all day doing the food for last night. I wanted to help so that she could have a rest.'

'I'm sure she was very pleased.'

'The rabbit, you know, in the shop . . . ' he coloured up again ' . . . When I said it was for my girlfriend, it was a fib. I haven't got a girlfriend. I wanted it for Carli.'

Janey turned to the sink and began washing the cutlery from her sandwich-making.

'Well, you'll soon have enough money to pay for the rabbit.' She didn't want to discuss that incident again. 'Now I must get ready to go to work.'

The China Dog

Janey arrived at the shop the next morning carrying a huge bunch of marguerites from her garden. Upstairs, in Martin's flat she filled two vases with the white daisies.

Pixie settled on her cushion and Janey went downstairs to open the shop. It was a fine morning and she prayed for some customers to boost her takings for the week. Her prayers were answered. Mrs Pryor from the cake shop came in looking for a small table lamp. Janey sent her away with a pretty Tiffany lamp which glowed red and green and gold when alight.

A young couple were searching for an old hall table. The girl was interested in the dolls'-house, but not enough to buy it. But they chose an oak table and went off well satisfied. Then the vicar arrived with the latest copy of the church magazine and left with a stone bird for his garden.

She closed the shop and went upstairs to eat her lunch and drink a welcome cup of coffee. When she'd finished, Pixie hopefully put a toy in her lap.

'No time for games. I have something important to do.'

She went to a cupboard in the kitchen and lifted out the cake tin in which she'd placed Martin's cake. When the lid was removed, there was a delicious smell of lemon.

In a short time she'd made a fluffy buttercream for the centre and then icing for the top.

She poured out on to a board a packet of sugar letters. On the iced top, she placed the words *WELCOME HOME, MARTIN.*

It wasn't until the cake was carefully put away and she'd had a quick game of tug-of-bone with Pixie, that she had time to think back over the night before.

It was the most enjoyable evening she'd had since coming to live in

Burntwood. Was that being disloyal to Martin? He'd taken her out often, even to parties, but she'd never enjoyed herself as she had with Ashe Corby. Why? Was she attracted to Ashe perhaps more than Martin? Ashe was attractive, different, exciting. Martin was too familiar. He held no mystery for her. She wanted to see Ashe again.

Ceri had warned her that at a party it meant nothing. But Janey couldn't believe that there wasn't a spark. She wondered when she would see him again. He knew she was at the shop. Perhaps he'd call in some time.

She went downstairs and through the glass door she could see the tall figure of a man. She pulled back the bolts and opened the door.

'Good afternoon, Janey. May I come in?'

'Ashe, what are you doing here?' Janey felt her cheeks hot with confusion. It was as if she'd summoned him up by magic.

'Love the dress,' he said.

'Martin's idea.' She giggled. 'But I like it, too.'

He lifted the bag he was carrying and put it on the counter. Then he began to unwrap the bundle and took out some beautiful, decorated china plates.

'I know they're old, but I wondered whether they were valuable. They were left to me by an aunt. They've been in a cupboard for years. Can you value them?'

'I'm afraid not. That's a skilled job. Martin can get them valued for you. He has lots of contacts.'

Ashe wrapped them up again.

'I'll leave them with you, then.' He walked towards the door rattling his car keys. 'I'd love to stay and have a look round, but I have to be at a meeting in an hour.'

Janey watched through the window as he drove off in a large black car. She put a hand to her cheek. Had he really been in the shop? Slowly, she walked over to the plates, carried them carefully to a cupboard at the back of the room and locked the door.

The telephone rang. It was Ceri.

'Have you recovered from last night?'

'It was wonderful. Guess who's just been in the shop?'

'No idea.'

'Ashe Corby. He wants some plates valued so he brought them in.'

'Sounds like an excuse.'

'You warned me about party romances.'

'Perhaps I was wrong. I hope so, for your sake.'

'He is nice.'

'And attractive and rich.'

'Ceri, that's not important.'

'Don't be crazy. Of course it's important. Anyway, I can't stay arguing with you. I must go back.'

'What are you doing now? Have you done any acting?'

'Just walking. Learning to walk in long heavy skirts, especially up and down stairs.'

'Oh. When shall I see you?'

'Don't know. I'll call you. Bye.'

A few sharp barks from the top of the

stairs reminded Janey that Pixie hadn't had her usual lunchtime stroll. She fastened Pixie's lead, locked the door and they set off up the street. As they passed the newsagents a man came out.

'Janey!' Kevin Shaw-Coles bent to pat Pixie, who snapped at his hand. The little Jack Russell had obviously made up her own mind about him. 'Doing anything tonight?'

Janey began to babble something about the garden.

'The garden won't run away. This time I won't take no for an answer. You're coming out to dinner with me.'

Janey gave in. He'd pester her until she did give in, so she might as well agree now.

'OK, yes, thank you.'

'Wonderful. I'll pick you up at seven.'

They parted and Janey walked back to the shop. Why had she agreed? She unlocked the door and they went in. Janey picked up a duster and went round the shop, polishing surfaces as she went.

She came to the collection of little animals and suddenly thought of Daniel. Was Ashe very strict with his son? She finished dusting and took the vacuum-cleaner from a cupboard. Over the noise of the engine she heard the shop bell ring. She flicked the *off* switch with her foot and turned to see who'd come in.

It was Daniel.

'Thank you for not mentioning the gardening to my father,' he said straight away.

'Perhaps he ought to know.'

'If you tell him, we can't do what you suggested. You know, take photos and so on.'

She shrugged.

'Let's just see what happens.'

'Can I do some work today?'

'Yes. But only for an hour.'

'I've only got an hour. I can't be too late for tea.'

'I'm leaving here now. You can walk down with me.'

Janey changed her dress and collected Pixie. Daniel's eyes shone when he saw the little dog.

'I'd like a dog,' he said wistfully.

'You can play with Pixie. Perhaps, when she knows you better, you can take her for walks.'

At the cottage, she took two bottles of orange juice from the fridge.

'Afraid I don't have any pop. Will this do?'

The boy sat down and shared a biscuit with the dog.

'Not too many. I don't want her to get fat.'

Pixie gave Janey a reproachful look. She obviously approved of the generous ways of her new friend.

'Come into the garden,' Janey said when they'd finished. 'We can see what else you can help me with. I'd like some help with mowing the lawn, trimming the hedges and a bit of digging. Not all today,' she added hastily. 'Take your time.'

'Do you have an electric mower?'

'Yes, a new one. It's in the shed.'

They crossed the garden and Janey

unlocked the shed.

The lawn was small and in half an hour it was cut to Daniel's satisfaction. He took some rags from the shed, cleaned the mower and replaced it in the shed. Janey went into the garden and found him a broom.

'Perhaps you could sweep the patio and the paths now.'

While he was working, she went up to her bedroom to review her outfit for the evening. Nothing too glamorous. She decided on jeans, a white silk T-shirt and a red cord jacket.

She went downstairs to find Daniel playing with Pixie. She took her purse from her bag. She and Daniel had already agreed an hourly rate. She took a note from her bag.

'If you take Pixie for a walk that will count, too,' she said as she handed over the money. 'Thank you for your hard work.'

Kevin was on time. He looked her over approvingly and held the car door open for her. She climbed in and they were soon heading into the country.

'Martin would be pleased. I promised him I'd keep an eye on you while he was away.'

Janey glanced at him with a feeling of annoyance.

'I'm capable of looking after myself.'

Kevin smiled but said nothing.

'Where are we going?'

'A new place, the China Dog. Have you heard of it?'

'No. What a strange name for a pub.'

'You'll see why when you get there. I shan't tell you. It's only about a mile away.'

They turned into one more lane and there, at the end, was the sign *THE CHINA DOG* with the picture of a white dog covered with black spots. They parked and strolled to the pub where a large door stood open and through which the sound of laughter could be heard.

'Sounds quite full,' Kevin warned. 'I hope we can get a table. They don't let you reserve one.'

The bar was full of people drinking and talking. Janey gazed at the wall behind the bar. It was covered with shelves full of china dogs: large white ones, medium-sized spotty ones, small black dogs, fat brown ones.

'There must be at least thirty,' she said.

'You just wait,' he replied and led the way to the dining-room. There were plenty of free tables and they chose one overlooking the garden. On the table were two tiny china dogs, one for salt, one for pepper.

The wall opposite the window was shelved like the bar and each shelf was covered with china dogs.

'Where on earth did they get them all from?'

'Apparently the owners have collected them for years and when they moved here, decided to use them as the theme for the pub.'

'Don't they lose any? You know, people might take them home as souvenirs.'

'A risk they're prepared to take, I suppose. Of course, they might be glued to the shelves!'

A waitress appeared and handed them each a menu.

'Are the lamb parcels on?' Kevin asked. 'Speciality of the house,' he explained to Janey. 'They're really good.'

They ordered the lamb parcels and a long cool drink.

Janey looked around at the spacious dining-room.

'It looks Swedish,' she said, 'you know, pale wood furniture and blue tablecloths and curtains.'

'Clever of you. Mine host's wife is Swedish.'

Their food arrived; small parcels of filo pastry containing spiced lamb and apricots. It was accompanied by fragrant pilaff rice.

Janey tasted it and smiled at Kevin.

'Gorgeous. The flavour is out of this world.'

Kevin looked pleased.

'I thought you'd like it. It's spicy but

not excessively so. Do you enjoy food?'

'Oh, yes, but I'm not an expert. I suppose I mostly eat good plain food. But I enjoy something like this.'

'It's one of my hobbies. I enjoy cooking and I enjoy eating out.'

They chatted about food and restaurants for a while and Janey was surprised to find herself enjoying the evening. Perhaps she had been too hasty in her judgement of Kevin.

They ate brandy baskets of fruit and cream and then ordered coffee.

Janey sat back with a sigh.

'What a wonderful meal.'

'Will you let me take you out again?'

'Martin will be back tomorrow. I don't know when I shall be free,' she prevaricated.

'You have to eat, even if Martin is home.'

Janey was silent for a few minutes. It was kind of Kevin to take her out, but she didn't want to tie up her evenings. Ashe had said he would ring to arrange dinner one evening and Martin would be sure to want to take her out to talk about his French trip. She smiled at Kevin.

'Could we leave it for a little while,' she suggested. She picked up her handbag. 'I really should be going. I have some writing to do this evening and tomorrow will be very busy.'

'Writing? Ah, yes. Martin mentioned your little books. Romances, aren't they?'

Janey took a deep breath. Why must people be so condescending about romance?

She stood up.

'Thank you for a delightful meal, Kevin. This place is a find.'

It was a beautiful evening.

'What about a stroll by the river?'

'I'm sorry,' she said firmly, 'I really need to go home.'

'So you won't be inviting me in for coffee?'

'Not this time,' she said with a forced laugh. She'd suddenly had enough of fending off Kevin Shaw-Coles. The sooner she was home the better.

At her gate he stopped the car, came round to her door and opened it. As she climbed out, he put his arms around her. Firmly she tried to remove them but he tightened his hold.

'Just one kiss,' he said thickly. 'Surely I deserve that.'

He tried to find her lips but she jerked her head away and he kissed her cheek.

A car came round the corner rather fast and Kevin, startled, released her. Janey whisked away from him and through the gate, closing it firmly.

'Thank you again, Kevin,' she said. 'I'll see you around.'

In a few minutes she was inside her house.

The meal was lovely, she thought, but the evening was a mistake. Next time he asked she would definitely refuse.

Surprise!

Janey replaced the phone handset and glanced round the flat. It looked bright and shining. The table was laid for tea; sandwiches, scones with jam and cream and in the centre, her lemon cake with the words, *WELCOME HOME, MARTIN.*

Satisfied, she picked up her car keys and flew down the stairs. The station was three minutes away. Martin was standing by a platform seat which was piled with cases and bags. Janey ran to him and flung her arms round his neck.

'I'm so pleased to see you. I have missed you.'

Martin held her close, then turned her towards the bench.

'Here's the surprise I promised you.'

At the far side of the pile of luggage sat a young woman. She was small and slight with a heart-shaped face and long, shining black hair.

Martin released Janey and put an arm around the girl.

'This is Amelie, my wife. Amelie, my friend, Janey.' The two girls looked at each other. Janey felt the colour drain from her face. His wife!

'I'm sorry.' The girl had a soft French accent. 'You are shocked. I tell Martin it is not good to keep it a secret.'

'No,' Janey hastened to reassure her. 'It's a lovely surprise. It's just that . . . ' She couldn't finish.

Martin began to pick up the cases and carry them to the car. The girls collected the bags and followed him.

Janey got into the driving seat, Martin sat beside her and Amelie climbed into the back. Janey tried to concentrate on Martin's chatter but found it hard to respond. She took a quick glance in the mirror at the French girl in the back of the car. Amelie said nothing but looked through the windows from side to side at her new surroundings. Martin turned and smiled over his shoulder at her.

'Nearly home,' he said cheerfully.

At the shop, Janey took Amelie upstairs while Martin unloaded the car. She showed the other girl where to hang her coat and pointed to the bathroom, then dashed into the dining-room. Carefully, with a sharp knife, she levered up the letters on the cake and brushed the marks with icing-sugar. Now it read, *WELCOME HOME*.

Martin and Amelie were hungry after their journey and appreciated Janey's tea.

'Janey is a really good cook.'

'I am not,' Amelie admitted. Janey had to smile at her woebegone little face.

'I'll teach you if you want to learn,' she offered.

She wanted to leave as soon as tea was finished but Martin wouldn't allow it.

'We've only just got back and you want to desert us. Tell me all that's happened while I've been away.'

Janey thought for a while.

74

'I went for dinner with Kevin,' she said.

'Good. He's a nice man, just right for you.'

She said nothing.

'What about sales? You told me about the Toby jug.'

'We'll talk about it tomorrow. I think your news is more important than anything I have to say!'

'My surprise, you mean?'

'Wasn't it rather sudden?'

'Amelie's father has a shop in Rouen. We met when I called there last year. We went out a few times and wrote to each other and, of course, phoned often.'

'I didn't know.'

'Why should you? When I went over this time, I spent most of my time in Rouen. Amelie's father was selling the enamelled boxes I was so keen to buy. We realised we were in love, got a special licence and were married last week.'

'And you said nothing.'

Martin looked a little discomfited.

'I'm sorry, Janey, I didn't realise it would upset you so much. I just thought the surprise would be fun.'

Janey stood up.

'Would you like to go and unpack while I wash these dishes? Then I really must go.'

Half an hour later she drove quickly away from the shop. She was desperate to be home.

Pixie's ecstatic welcome soothed her a little.

'You love me, don't you?' Janey sank to the floor and cradled the soft little body in her arms. 'I thought I was going to have a good cry when I got home, but I don't feel like crying. Why is that?'

Pixie leaped off her lap and looked at her hopefully.

'Good idea.' Janey got to her feet and took the dog's lead from the hook. 'A walk.'

She let herself out of the cottage and they set off down the road. It was a beautiful evening full of flower scents and birdsong. Far too pleasant to be miserable.

The road forked at the end. One way led to the forest. She decided not to go there. If she met Ashe he might think she was looking for him.

She turned into the other road. Large houses fronted by flower-filled gardens lined each side of the road. Dr Shepherd lived at the end and Janey was pleased to see his wife, Margaret, dead-heading her rose bushes.

'Janey, dear! Are you coming to see us?'

'Well, I was really taking Pixie for a walk, but I'm glad you're around. I have some news for you.'

'Come along. We'll have a drink and you can tell us what it is. Tom,' she called to her husband, 'look who I've found. She has some news for us.'

Dr Shepherd had been reading the newspaper in the conservatory at the back of the house, but he came through at his wife's voice.

'Janey, how nice to see you.' He put

77

an arm round her shoulders. 'Pixie can go into the garden. She'll enjoy some different smells.' He opened the garden door.

'Pour us a drink,' his wife said, 'and Janey can tell us her news. I hope it's good.'

Janey looked at their expectant faces.

'Martin has come back from France — married.'

'Married? To whom?' He wasn't engaged, was he?'

'No. She's French. He's known her for about a year.'

'And he said nothing.' Margaret looked dismayed. 'How do you feel about it?'

Janey thought for a moment.

'I love Martin, he's been so good to me, but I'm beginning to realise that I was never in love with him. And he obviously doesn't love me. So I'll accept it and move on. Amelie is very sweet,' she added.

Dr Shepherd and his wife exchanged glances.

'That's a sensible way to look at it. You're young and the world is full of young men. You'll find someone soon.'

'She might have already found someone,' the doctor said with a mysterious smile.

'Really? Who can that be? You don't mean Kevin Shaw-Coles?' There was a hint of disapproval in Margaret's voice.

'No,' Janey said forcefully. 'Certainly not.'

Margaret relaxed.

'I'm glad. I don't know him very well but one hears things. I shouldn't like to see you hurt by that young man.'

She looked at her husband.

'What do you think of Ashe Corby?' he said.

'You're being a gossip.' Janey glared. 'I've only met him a few times.'

'He's very nice,' Margaret mused. 'Older than you.'

'That's not a bad fault,' the doctor said. 'I think he'd do very nicely for Janey.'

Janey stood up.

'Thank you for arranging my future. Now I must go home and do some writing!'

Dr Shepherd and Margaret walked with her to the gate.

'Bring Amelie next week,' Margaret said. 'I should love to meet her. Then we can fix up a date for dinner.'

Janey walked home in a more cheerful frame of mind. She meant what she'd said to the Shepherds. She really didn't mind about Martin's marriage. But whether she'd decided that because of Ashe Corby she wasn't sure.

Back at Pippin Cottage, she settled down to work on her manuscript. She smiled to herself as she remembered how she'd thought of using Ashe as her villain.

She closed her eyes and visualised the next scene.

The hero strode into the heroine's drawing-room. He was tall, wide-shouldered and had a quiff of hair falling over one eye.

A few days later, when Janey reached the shop, she found Martin and Amelie in a state of great excitement.

'We've decided to have a party,' Martin told her. 'I want to introduce my wife to all my friends. Do you think tomorrow would be too soon?'

'A bit of a rush. Were you thinking of having it here?'

'That would mean Amelie, or probably you ... ' he smiled at Janey ' ... making all the preparations. No, if they're free, we'll book a room at the Golden Fleece. They'll do the catering and we'll just have to turn up.'

Martin bounded off and Amelie smiled at Janey.

'A party is nice, but I shall feel nervous.'

'They'll be pleased Martin has found someone.'

The French girl fingered a turquoise bracelet.

'I think you know a lot about antiques. Martin said you are a great help to him. Me, I don't know very much.' Again she looked downcast.

'Your father has several antiques shops, hasn't he?'

'Yes, but I was at college.'

'What were you studying?'

'I wanted to be a teacher. Of small children.'

Janey could see Amelie with little children. She seemed childlike herself.

Martin came back into the room.

'They have a free room on Thursday evening. But they want to discuss the catering. Will you go, Janey?'

'We'll both go.' Janey smiled at Amelie. 'But first we must make a list of guests, then you can phone people.'

Between them they made a list of 40 people.

'Cater for fifty, just to be sure,' Martin said. 'You'd better start phoning. Come along, Amelie.'

Janey found the business of organising the party quite fun. Amelie wasn't much help, but seemed happy to tag along to the hotel and let Janey make the decisions.

When they'd inspected the room and discussed the menu they were given coffee and biscuits in the garden. Amelie leaned back in her reclining seat and closed her eyes.

'It is so nice to sit here and feel the sun on my face.'

'You'll miss the sun, although we sometimes have very hot weather. Let's hope this summer will be hot for you.'

Amelie sat up and looked shyly at Janey.

'Do you dislike me for marrying Martin?'

'Why should I?'

'Perhaps you have a sweetheart?'

'No.' Janey gave a little laugh. 'I don't want one. I'm working hard at my writing. I want to be famous one day.'

'Ah, yes. Martin gave me one of your books. I think you are a very clever person. You can look after the shop and cook and write books. Why did not Martin marry you?'

'Because we were not in love.'

'I hope Martin loves me,' Amelie said

in a small voice.

Janey was startled.

'Whatever do you mean?'

Amelie gave a little shrug and walked a little way off.

Back at the shop, Martin was assiduously working his way through the guest list.

'I've managed to contact a number of people. Almost everyone has accepted. Is everything OK at the hotel?'

'We've told the hotel that we'll do the flowers,' Janey said. 'I think Amelie could do them very well.'

The French girl gave her a grateful smile.

'Thank you. Maman says I am very good with flowers.'

'Phone Ceri and see if she can come,' Martin said to Janey, 'and anyone else you'd like to invite.'

What would he say if she turned up with Ashe?

★　★　★

When Janey reached Pippin Cottage, Daniel was hard at work trimming a bush with a large pair of scissors.

'What are you doing?' Janey asked with a laugh. 'There are shears in the shed.'

'Too big. Scissors are best.'

'But what are you doing?'

'Can't you see? You have to use some imagination.'

Janey looked at the bush again.

'No, I'm sorry, you just seem to be cutting a bush with some scissors. I can't imagine why.'

'I'm making a bird.' Daniel snipped away industriously. 'It'll probably look more like one in a few weeks.'

'Oh, I see.' Janey tried not to smile. To her the bush still looked like a bush. 'I'll get you a drink.'

In the kitchen she stood looking out of the window. Daniel had made quite a difference in a few visits. The lawn was neat and short, hedges had been trimmed and the terrace kept swept and clean.

She felt a twinge of conscience. Perhaps she should tell Ashe, just casually as if it was no big deal. But Ashe might forbid him to do it. Daniel would be devastated.

When Daniel had left, she phoned Ceri's number several times but her flatmate answered.

'I'm afraid she's away.'

'I thought she was filming.'

'She is, in Wales. For some of the castle scenes. Did you want her for anything special?'

'No. Just a chat. I'll ring next week.'

She replaced the phone and looked at Pixie.

'Do you want your dinner or a walk first?'

The little dog scampered to the door.

'You don't hear anything except the word walk, do you?' Janey asked. 'Very well.'

She fastened the lead and they left the cottage and set off. At the crossroads, Janey hesitated. Which way?

Before she could decide, a tall man

coming from the direction of the forest came near enough for recognition.

'Well, Red Riding Hood, how nice to see you. Were you coming to see me? It's quite a walk.'

'We were just going for a stroll,' she said. 'I'm deciding which way to go.'

'What about coming to the butts?' he asked. 'I'll give you a guided tour.' He held her arm as they crossed the road. They entered the forest and started down the path where they had first met.

At the end of the path, the forest opened into a clearing. Before them stood four large sheets of wood, side by side.

'Are those the butts?'

'Yes. We hang the targets on them.'

'Is that your clubhouse?' Janey pointed to a scruffy small building at the side.

'That's a grand name for it. We call it the Hut. Would you like a cup of coffee?' Ashe took some keys from his pocket and unlocked the door. It had been furnished with everyone's cast-off furniture: a battered wooden table littered with tools and feathers, two armchairs with stuffing oozing out of the side and a reasonably comfortable-looking sofa. On another table stood a blackened paraffin stove and some chipped crockery. Leaning against the far wall was a pile of targets. There was a lingering smell of leather, beeswax, woodshavings and oil.

Ashe led the way outside again.

'You don't just shoot here, do you?' Janey asked. 'I've seen some other targets through the trees.'

'Mm. Twenty-six in all. Some through the trees, some across streams. Different lengths, of course. You'll have to come one day when we're practising.'

'I'd like that, but now I think I should go back.'

'Did your boss arrive home safely?' Ashe asked.

For a moment, Janey had forgotten Amelie and Martin.

'Yes. He brought me a surprise. A wife.'

Ashe stood still and looked at her.

'A wife? That was a shock, not a surprise, wasn't it?'

'At first, yes. But I've accepted it. And I like Amelie.'

'It seems an inconsiderate thing to do to you.'

'Martin and I are friends, but nothing more.'

Ashe changed the subject.

'Have you decided when you'll come out with me?'

She smiled up at him.

'Would you like to come to a party? It's for Martin and Amelie's wedding. For her to meet Martin's friends. He told me to bring any of my friends I liked.'

'I'm honoured. And yes, I'd love to come. When is it?'

'The day after tomorrow, at the Golden Fleece.'

They had reached the road.

'I'll be there,' he said. 'I look forward to it.'

Dressed To Impress

When Daniel arrived the next morning Janey was working hard at her manuscript. She was glad to see him. He could solve a problem for her.

'Could you be very kind and take Pixie for a walk? I really want to get on with my book. When you get an idea you need to get it down as soon as possible.'

Pixie, who'd heard the word walk, was bouncing up and down near the hook which held her lead.

'Take her up on to the common.'

When they'd gone, Janey settled down and wrote steadily for an hour. The story was coming on very well. She was pleased with her choice of Ashe as the hero. His handsome face was before her as she wrote.

When Daniel and Pixie returned, Janey made drinks and produced chocolate biscuits. Pixie begged for one in vain.

'We don't want fat little dogs round here,' Janey said, pouring a few dog biscuits into Pixie's bowl.

She looked at Daniel.

'I've been thinking of how you're going to persuade your father to let you take up horticulture. What if we took photographs of my garden as it is now, and then you drew up a plan of how you would change it, worked on it, then we photographed the result? He could hardly deny that you're keen if he saw all that effort.'

'Would you really let me alter your garden?'

'Why not? I don't mind how it looks as long as it is attractive.'

Daniel was thinking hard.

'It's a cracking idea,' he said at last. 'I'll see what I can come up with.'

He ate the biscuit thoughtfully.

'You really are a friend, Janey.'

She smiled at him, pleased.

'Here's a pad.' Janey unearthed a

notepad from under a pile of magazines. 'Take this pencil and measuring tape and make a start.'

She went back to her writing. At the back of her mind was the worry that Ashe might see her actions as interference. She opened her dictionary. She'd deal with Ashe when the time came.

★ ★ ★

Janey decided not to be the first to arrive at the party. Amelie and Martin could check things and greet their guests without her help. After all, it was their party.

She spent a long time over her appearance, soaking in a bubble bath until she felt her skin must be thoroughly impregnated with the lovely honey and vanilla scent. She reached for her dress. Ceri had first spotted the dress in the window of Burntwood's only expensive boutique.

'I wish I could wear that colour,' she moaned, pointing to the gleaming bronze dress. 'Isn't it gorgeous!'

Janey agreed. She made to walk on.

'It would look wonderful on you.'

Janey examined the price ticket.

'I can't spend that on a dress,' she exclaimed. 'And where would I wear it? Ceri, you're crazy!'

'It's the dress you keep in your wardrobe for just the right occasion. Try it on.' She was urging her friend towards the shop door as she spoke. And somehow Janey found herself, 20 minutes later, carrying the dress in a large bag with an exclusive logo on the front.

Now she was pleased Ceri had persuaded her. The dress fitted as if it had been made for her. She fastened pearl drop earrings into her earlobes. She swirled her hair softly on to her head and carefully made up her face. Now, as she examined her reflection, she felt satisfied that she could measure up to what she was sure were Ashe's standards.

He was used to London fashions and

film glamour. She mustn't look like a country mouse.

Martin came face to face with her when she entered the room in the Golden Fleece where the party was in full swing.

'Wow! Janey, you look magnificent.'

Behind him, Amelie stared.

'Janey, you look so chic, so elegant,' she breathed.

The girls linked arms.

'Have you met Martin's friends?'

'Many people. I like the doctor and his wife very much. They said we must go to dinner with them very soon.'

Janey took her back into the party. She was conscious that some people were watching them, calculating whether she really was friendly with Martin's new wife or whether it was an act. The doctor and his wife were not the only people to have expected Martin to marry her.

The music started. Martin claimed his wife. Kevin Shaw-Coles appeared behind him.

'Shall we dance?'

Over his shoulder, she'd spotted someone in the doorway of the room. Ashe!

She gave Kevin a distracted smile.

'Later, Kevin. I've just seen someone.'

She moved towards the door. Ashe's face broke into a wide smile as he recognised her.

'Janey! Words fail me.'

'You made it. I was beginning to wonder whether you'd changed your mind.'

'I didn't want to arrive too early, when perhaps you weren't here. Shall we dance?'

She shook her head.

'I can't for the moment. I've just refused someone else. And of course I must introduce you to Amelie and Martin.'

They were seated in one of the alcoves at the side of the room. She noticed Martin looking at her. Of course he didn't know Ashe. Taking Amelie's hand, he crossed the room to where they were sitting.

Janey introduced them. Ashe smiled easily at Amelie and addressed a few words to her in French which delighted her. Martin watched him warily.

'So, where did you two meet?'

'In the forest. I was taking Pixie for a walk. Then later, Ceri took me to a party for the film company and it was held at Ashe's house. So we met again.'

'I see.' Martin was plainly not happy. 'Have you danced with Kevin? He was looking for you. Here he is.'

'I've come to claim my dance.' Kevin slipped an arm round Janey's waist.

She turned an apologetic face to Ashe.

'Don't worry about me. I see Doctor Tom over there. I'll chat to him while you finish dancing.'

Janey went off reluctantly with Kevin.

'I didn't know you knew Ashe Corby.'

'Why should you? Do you know him?'

'I know of him. Business man. Plays with bows and arrows in his spare time.'

'He's a very good archer, among other things. He's advising on fight scenes in a film.'

'He's impressed you, anyway.' Kevin gave a spiteful little laugh.

'The music's stopped. I'm going to get a drink.'

'Allow me.' Kevin took her arm.

She gently disengaged it.

'No, thank you, Kevin. I can manage on my own.' She moved swiftly between the dancers and over to Ashe.

'Shall we get a drink? Dancing is thirsty work.'

'You didn't look as if you were enjoying it.'

Janey sighed.

'I wasn't. Mr Shaw-Coles is not my favourite person.'

'But you are his.'

'He's Martin's best friend, so it's difficult.'

'Shall we take our drinks outside?'

They found a bench set against a

border of night-scented stocks. The perfume was intoxicating.

Janey closed her eyes.

'What a lovely evening.' A faint breeze cooled her warm cheeks. 'It's so refreshing out here.'

'Where is your friend, Ceri?'

'Filming in Wales, I believe.'

'Of course. The company is there for two weeks. Then we do a few scenes in the forest. Would you like to watch?'

'May I? Yes, I should love that.'

Ashe finished his drink.

'What about that dance?' He stood up, held out a hand to Janey and pulled her to her feet.

Her ankle went over as she stepped on an uneven stone and it threw her off balance. Ashe swung an arm round her waist and pulled her towards him. She turned her face up to his and he lightly kissed the end of her nose.

'Come on, Red Riding Hood, let's go in.'

Near the door, a man paced up and down smoking. It was Kevin. The look he gave them wasn't friendly.

The dance floor was still crowded, but they found a small space and began to move to the music. Held firmly in his arms, Janey gave herself up to the gentle rhythm.

He smiled down at her.

'Happy?'

'Oh, yes. Are you?'

'At this moment, perfectly.'

The dance over, a voice said that supper was served.

'Thank goodness. I'm starving. It's not very ladylike to admit that, is it?'

'At least you're honest.'

Supper was delicious. As soon as the music started up again, they went back to the dance floor.

Martin appeared.

'May I have a dance, Janey?'

Amelie was just behind him, looking lost. Ashe immediately held out a hand to her and without a word, they joined the dancers.

'You seem very involved with your friend,' Martin said.

'Involved? What do you mean?'

'You've spent almost every minute with him. How long have you known him?'

'Not long. Martin, you have a wife to worry about now. Don't try to control me. I'm a big girl now.'

'He must be at least ten years older than you.'

'And you? I'm sure you're ten years older than Amelie.'

'Eight, actually.'

They danced in silence again. They passed Amelie and Ashe who were deep in conversation.

'Janey, I might be married, but it won't make any difference to us, will it?'

'What do you mean to us?'

'We were close friends. I don't want that to change.'

'I don't want it to change, either,' she replied. 'I hope I shall always be a close friend . . . of you and Amelie.'

The music stopped and Janey was glad to lead the way back to their table. Ashe and Amelie were already there.

'Come along,' Martin said to her in a brusque tone of voice. 'We must arrange to have the wedding gifts packed to take home.' Without another word he led her away.

Ashe gave Janey a rueful smile.

'He doesn't like me. Is he jealous?'

Janey looked thoughtful.

'I don't understand him. He chose to get married. I'm free to do as I like.'

'And would you like another dance?'

'I would!'

★　★　★

Martin greeted her quite naturally when she arrived at Forge Antiques the next morning and showed no sign of his pique of the night before. He was showing Amelie how to dust some of the more delicate pieces of porcelain with a tiny feather duster.

'Could you make us all a cup of coffee?'

Amelie disappeared upstairs.

'You've got her working quickly.'

'She's got a lot to learn. I can't understand why she knows so little about the business.'

'Amelie wanted to be a nursery teacher. You'll have to start from the beginning with antiques. Try patience.'

She went into the office and quickly changed into her long pink and white striped dress.

Amelie returned with the coffee.

'I enjoyed the party so much last night,' she said to Janey. 'Thank you for all your help.'

Janey waited for a comment about Ashe, but nothing came. She finished her coffee and spent the next half hour in the office. She came back into the shop as the bell on the door gave a tinkle. The door opened and Ashe came in.

Martin spun round. Janey caught an expression of annoyance, instantly replaced by an insincere smile.

'How nice to see you again so soon.'

Ashe walked up to Martin with his hand extended.

'I've come to thank you for a pleasant evening.'

Martin shook hands.

'Do look round if you'd like to, or have you already done that when I was away?'

'No. I popped in for a few minutes, but I had an appointment. There wasn't time to look around.'

She stepped forward.

'I've mentioned your plates, Ashe. He's going to get them valued, aren't you, Martin?'

'I'll take them over to Reg Driver next week. He's the best valuer in the area,' he said to Ashe.

'Have you a few minutes to talk?' Ashe asked Janey. 'I just wanted to say that, if it's convenient, I'd like to take you to watch some filming next Wednesday.'

'Thank you. I'd love to come.'

Ashe looked her up and down.

'Now, which do I prefer, the simple village maid in pink and white or the elegant lady in bronze taffeta?'

'Which should I wear to watch the filming?'

'Jeans and a warm jacket. It might be cold.'

When he'd gone, Martin looked at her curiously.

'He wants to take me to watch some filming in the forest. Would it be OK if I took Wednesday morning off?'

'Do you know what you're doing? You don't know anything about this man except you met him in the forest!'

'Which he owns.' Janey's voice was defiant.

'What did you say?'

'He inherited the forest last year. He also owns a house at the end of it. Dr Shepherd is a friend of his.'

Martin looked thoughtful.

'Well, if he's a friend of Tom Shepherd . . . '

'So, is it all right about Wednesday morning?'

'Yes, of course.' Martin walked away. 'I'm just going downstairs to sort that box of cutlery.'

Sword F...

The following Wednesday, ...
to Ashe's house at what seem...
unearthly hour. He'd told her th...
filming always started early.

Ashe came out of the house as she
drove up.

'Come and have some breakfast first.'

There was no sign of Daniel. Janey
didn't ask where he was. Mrs Carlson
gave her a friendly greeting and put a
tray of warm croissants and a pot of
coffee in front of them.

When they'd eaten they went back
outside and climbed into Ashe's battered Land-Rover.

'Just the thing for forest tracks,' he
said as he loaded bows and arrows and
mysterious-looking boxes into the vehicle.
Soon they were jolting and swaying down
a very uneven path and into the depths
of the forest.

is the oldest part. It has some
rful ancient oak trees just right
ur purpose.'

net assumed he meant the film.

The trees opened out into a large
clearing where chaos reigned. It was full
of people: people sitting, standing,
climbing trees, manning cameras and
lighting equipment. There were girls in
long skirts and men in long boots.
Several young woman darted here and
there with lists and clip boards, looking
harassed. At the edge, a group of horses
munched at a patch of grass.

A man came towards them. Janey
recognised Wynn, the director, from the
party at Ashe's house. He greeted them
warmly.

'We made a good start yesterday,'
he told Ashe, 'but I've left all the fight
scenes for today. Don't know how
much we'll get done.'

'How is young Kyle shaping up?'

'His riding is superb but I don't
know about anything else. You'll have to
work on him today. But be firm. I'm

afraid he's a young show-off.'

Janey waved to Ceri who was with a group of girls sitting under a tree.

Wynn pointed to some chairs.

'Find a seat, Miss Robbins. I hope there'll be something for you to watch soon.'

Wynn hurried off, his mind already on ten other things.

'I'm rather worried about you now you're here,' Ashe said. 'I shan't be able to stay with you. I'll be all over the place.'

'Please, don't worry, I'll be fine here. There's so much to watch. Don't think about me.'

Ashe grasped her shoulder and squeezed it.

'I'll be back at lunchtime if not before. Now I'll go and find young Kyle.'

Janey was engrossed in watching a group of village women arguing with the Sheriff of Nottingham, when the sound of swords clashing behind her made her spin round.

In a clearing behind her chair, Ashe and Kyle were furiously fighting with swords as if to the death. Ashe called out instructions as they fought. Then they stopped and another costumed figure nearby took Ashe's place and the fight went on as before. When Ashe called a halt, they all took copious swigs of water from very twentieth-century-looking bottles hidden behind a nearby tree.

The two young men sat exhausted on the ground, while Ashe, who didn't seem to be tired out by the exertion, demonstrated various moves to them.

The director appeared and spoke to Ashe. Then he dismissed the others and Ashe joined Janey.

'That was marvellous!' She turned to him with shining eyes. 'Why aren't you in the film? You're miles better than all of them.'

'I'm not an actor,' he said, flinging himself into a chair next to her. 'I haven't the time or the inclination. For me it's a hobby.'

'Kyle is good, isn't he?'

'You know him?'

'Not really. But he was at the party with Ceri.'

'Of course. Yes, he has the makings of a good fencer. This afternoon I'll see how his archery has progressed.'

'Are they going to do any filming today?'

'Oh, yes. They've done some already. They'll probably shoot the scene we've just rehearsed. I think it's ready. Would you like some coffee?'

'Yes, please.'

He stood up, stretched, and pulled Janey to her feet.

'I can do with some myself. Come along, the catering truck is over there.'

They returned to their seats with mugs of coffee, but almost immediately Ashe was taken away by one of the bossy young women with a clipboard.

Janey looked around and was pleased to see that Ceri had left her group and was hurrying towards her.

'Ceri!' Janey patted the seat next to

her. 'Can you talk?'

'Yes. Short break.'

'Good. Isn't all this facinating?' Janey waved a hand to take in the scene. 'I don't know where to look first.'

Ceri glanced carelessly over her shoulder.

'You soon take it for granted. Have you seen any shooting yet?'

'Shooting? No, only fencing. Oh, I see what you mean.' She laughed. 'You mean filming. No, Ashe says that's for this afternoon.'

'Ashe?' Ceri gave her a knowing smile.

'Yes, he brought me. How's your romance with Kyle.'

'It's not a romance — yet.' Ceri coloured a little. 'But he looks so gorgeous in that costume, I can't stop looking at him.'

'Ashe says he's a very good fencer,' Janey told her.

'Does he?' Cari was pleased. 'I wish I had a scene with him, but I'm not important and he's the star.'

'So you keep your scenes for off the film.'

'I wish.' Ceri looked gloomy. 'We've had two dates, but there are so many girls in this film . . . '

Janey, watching her, saw Ceri's expression change to a bright smile. Kyle was approaching and had obviously come to speak to Ceri.

He gave Janey a brief greeting. He doesn't recognise me, she thought.

'Coffee, Ceri?'

Ceri jumped to her feet and, with a glance at Janey, was off in the direction of the catering truck.

Filming started again. There was no chance to watch Ashe in action as a fencer; he stood out of range and encouraged Kyle and the actor he was fighting.

The director, Wynn, seemed pleased and Janey saw him clap Ashe on the back. The actors jumped on to their horses and rode off into the trees.

Ashe appeared at her side.

'We can go now. I'm sure you're fed

up with this noise and showing off.'

'Not fed up at all, but I am rather stiff,' she admitted. 'I'm not used to sitting for so long. But I have enjoyed it. What happened to the archery?'

'They're not ready for that yet,' he said as they climbed into the Land-Rover. 'By the way, are you free this evening?'

'Free? Yes.'

'Will you have dinner with me?'

Janey looked down at her clothes.

'I'm not dressed to go out to dinner. Another night?'

'I'll run you home first. I need to change, too.'

'In that case, thank you.'

Ashe dropped her at the cottage and promised to be back in an hour.

There was no Pixie to hold her up, she was at her second home, a cottage halfway down the road where an elderly lady, Mrs Parsloe, doted on her.

Janey dashed upstairs, showered and gave her hair a vigorous brushing. Then she pulled a soft teal-coloured skirt from the wardrobe and found her white cowl-necked jumper.

Ten minutes later, dressed and made-up, she stood at the window waiting for Ashe. He was on time and gave her an admiring glance as she hurried down the path to his car.

'What a transformation,' he said as she entered the car. 'You look lovely.'

'Where are we going?'

'Do you know the Ferry Boat?'

'I've heard of it but I've never been there.'

Probably because it was one of the most expensive places in the county. Martin had taken her to some very nice restaurants but not the Ferry Boat.

They pulled up in the car park of a small building facing the river.

'There was a rope ferry here at one time.'

Janey looked up at the building. It was obviously old and creeper covered most of the front.

'I thought it would be bigger than this.'

'Good things come in small parcels, as my mother use to say. I don't think you'll be disappointed with the inside.'

The rooms were small but exquisitely furnished, almost like a country house. Polished wood, chintz sofas and gleaming brass was everywhere. Ashe led her through the reception hall to a dining-room facing the river. Through the wide windows they could see tables and umbrellas.

'We could eat outside if you like,' he suggested.

She looked around the pleasant dining-room.

'I think I'd prefer it here. It might get cold later on.'

They chose a table in the window and were soon studying the small, hand-written menus.

'The choice is not large,' he said, 'but everything is beautifully cooked and presented. I'm sure you'll enjoy whatever you choose.'

'What are you having?'

'I shall have whatever you're having,'

he said, placing his menu on the table.

She stared at him, wide-eyed.

'But what if I choose something you don't like?'

'You won't. I shall like what you like.'

'I shall have duck,' she said defiantly.

'A perfect choice. I enjoy duck.'

'And to start, I shall have pepper Stilton mushrooms.'

'Good. Just what I would have chosen myself.'

'I don't believe you,' she said with a giggle. 'But you'll have to eat it now.'

He gave the order to the waiter and then consulted with the wine waiter. Janey watched through the window as a mother moorhen shepherded a crowd of baby chicks towards the opposite bank.

'How did you enjoy today?'

'It was most interesting. But I shouldn't like to be involved in filming myself.'

'Why not?'

'Well, there's too much standing around. I like to be occupied.'

'Even when they're standing around, as you put it, they're busy. But I know what you mean. It wouldn't do for me either.'

'But you are involved in it.'

'Only occasionally. It's my hobby, not my career. I prefer to be busy in the city.'

Their food arrived and filming was forgotten as Janey applied herself to the delicious first course.

'When are they filming the archery?' she asked when they'd finished.

'Some tomorrow, some later on near the castle.'

'Is Kyle a good archer?'

Ashe made a face.

'Not as good as he is at fencing. We'll probably have to mock it up a bit. The camera will be on him but I'll fire the arrows.'

'So you'll be in the film after all.'

'But I shan't be seen,' he said with a laugh. 'That's the way I like it.'

Their duck arrived garnished with orange segments and watercress. Janey felt her mouth water as the aroma of orange, brandy and caramel wafted from the plate.

'Bigarade sauce, madam,' the waiter said, observing the expression an her face.

Janey gave him a smile.

'I'm sure it will taste as good as it smells.'

At the end of the meal, she felt she had never eaten so well before.

Ashe nodded towards her empty plate.

'It obviously did taste good.'

'It was superb.' Janey dabbed at her lips with her napkin. 'How can I ever eat frozen duck pieces from the supermarket again?'

Ashe smiled and refilled her wine glass.

'How are things settling down at Forge Antiques?' he asked. 'Is it a problem having a new wife there?'

Janey considered.

'No. Amelie and I get on very well. But I'm afraid that Martin will continue to lean on me and I feel that his wife should really take my place.'

'Does Amelie know a lot about antiques?'

'That's the problem. Although her father owns several antique shops, she's never shown much interest. She was training to be a nursery teacher when Martin met her.'

'Perhaps she could continue to do that and you could continue to be second in command at the shop. Oh, sorry. I'm sorting out your futures for you.'

Janey waved a hand.

'Not at all, everything has to be considered. No, Amelie wants to learn about antiques. She wants to work with Martin. And I shouldn't mind taking a back seat and concentrating on my writing.'

'You've had some books published, haven't you? You're not a beginner.'

'I've had five published so far,' she replied with a touch of pride. 'But I need to get a bestseller before I can think of writing as a full-time career.'

The waiter appeared with the menu. Ashe chose the cheese board and Janey decided on tiny strawberry tarts.

'You've mentioned your business in town. What sort of business is it?'

'Property development. Rather special property. We find houses for people, often celebrities, who may be spending just weeks or months in England and want somewhere special to live. We buy up and modernise properties all over England.'

'Do you have any celebrities on your books at the moment, or is that confidential?'

He thought.

'My most famous client at the moment, I'm sure she won't mind me telling you, is Maria Marchant.'

'Maria Marchant? The American film star. Wow!'

'Wow, indeed.' He smiled. 'She's very grand and very rich. She will be filming in England for five months and wants something like a 'little old castle', as she puts it.'

'Do you have any on your books?'

'Oh, yes. But I think she really means an historic manor house. We're having discussions at the moment.'

'Is she as beautiful as she looks in her films?'

'Certainly. And very nice, too. A sense of her own importance, but I like her.'

Janey thought of Ashe mixing with people like Maria Marchant. It was even more puzzling why he wanted to spend time with her. Surely he could find a more glamorous dinner companion.

Ashe stood up, interrupting her reverie.

'Let's have coffee in the conservatory.'

Afterwards, Janey found it difficult to remember what they had discussed. They sat for an hour with their coffee and chatted continuously. They had no difficulty in finding topics and seemed in accord on most of them.

Janey was startled to realise it was

well after ten o'clock when she looked at her watch.

'I think we must go now. We both have things to do tomorrow. It's been lovely.'

They walked slowly across the car park. Ashe slipped an arm round her waist. They stopped at the river bank and gazed at the water.

'What a lovely evening. Just listen to the silence.'

Ashe didn't laugh at her.

'I know what you mean. I love the countryside at night. Some evenings I walk in the forest just to listen to the silence.'

There was another car parked not far away. A couple were walking towards it, the girl laughing noisily. The peace was broken.

Ashe took out his keys and opened the door. Janey was about to slip inside when the other man spoke.

'Good evening, Janey. Did you enjoy your meal?'

She spun round. Kevin Shaw-Coles.

The last person she wanted to see her with Ashe.

'It was perfect, thank you,' she said, and was inside before he could continue the conversation.

Ashe swung into his seat, started the engine and they were out of the car park before Kevin's car could move.

'I gather you didn't want to stay and chat.'

'That dreadful man. He haunts me,' Janey said. 'Why did he have to be here?'

'At least we didn't see him in the dining-room. That might have spoiled your meal.'

'Don't let's talk about him. When are you going to Wales to film the archery bits?'

'In a few days. I can only be there for three days. What a pity you can't come, too. You'd enjoy it.'

'I don't think it would be a good idea. Beside, I have to help Martin and Amelie. And write,' she added. 'I have a deadline to meet.'

They drove on in silence. It was quite dark now. Janey watched the headlights slicing through the darkness ahead.

Three days in Wales with Ashe. What a wonderful thought! But not a good idea. People would talk and Martin would have a fit.

But she could dream about it.

They turned into her road and stopped outside Pippin Cottage. Ashe opened her door and accompanied her up the path to her front door. He took the key from her hand, fitted it into the lock and opened the door.

All the while, Janey's thoughts were in a turmoil. Should she just say goodbye, or ask him in for a drink?

Ashe looked down at her upturned face then he bent forward and gently kissed her lips.

'Goodnight, Janey.' His voice was husky. 'Thank you for your company. I've really enjoyed today.'

She gazed up at him.

'I've enjoyed it, too,' she whispered.

There was a pause of a second then

his arms were around her and this time the kiss was not gentle but hard and passionate. Then he stepped away from her.

'Goodnight, Janey,' he said again, and was gone.

Janey drifted into the cottage and closed the door. She touched her mouth with her fingertips.

She could still feel the imprint of his lips.

The Broken Plate

Janey could hear raised voices before she opened the door of Forge Antiques. Martin and Amelie had only been married for a short while, but the first flush of marital happiness seemed to be wearing off very quickly. Several times lately she'd heard them arguing over things which seemed quite unimportant — the way a new display was arranged or whether Amelie had dusted the porcelain ladies carefully enough.

'Watch Janey!' Martin was always shouting. 'She does things properly. Learn from her.'

Then he would storm out of the shop or disappear into the cellar.

This morning the argument seemed more bitter than usual.

'I have tried to copy Janey, but you are never satisfied with what I do!' the French girl sobbed. 'Janey has been helping you for a long time. I will learn if you give me time.'

'I can't understand why you don't know anything about antiques,' Martin said.

'Antiques were my father's interest, not mine. But I am trying hard to learn. You are so impatient.'

Janey, embarrassed to be listening to their argument, crept out of the shop then returned, banging the door.

Amelie looked at her, eyes red with weeping. Then without a word, she rushed up the stairs.

'What's the matter with Amelie?' Janey walked past Martin to the office.

He moved quietly after her and caught her hand.

'This isn't working. Amelie is hopeless. I only need you to help me.'

'Amelie is your wife. She loves you and she wants to be part of the business. You can't shut her out.' Janey pulled her hand free.

'But you and I work so well together. I don't need Amelie.'

'Martin!' Janey was horrified. 'If you talk like that I'll leave now and find another job. In fact, I might find somewhere else to live.'

As she said this she felt a cold sensation in her stomach. Leave her dear little cottage. Could she do it, for Amelie and Martin's marriage?

She could and she would. Lately she'd had the feeling that Martin didn't really love his wife. That he was already regretting the marriage. All her sympathy was for the French girl who so obviously loved her husband.

She went into the office, closed the door and changed into her striped dress. Martin was unreasonable. Then a thought struck her. If she left, he would probably blame Amelie.

The other girl would be even more unhappy. She resolved to stay and try to do something about the situation.

Perhaps she could spend more time helping the other girl. She opened the office door. Martin was still in the corridor outside. She walked past him and up the stairs.

Amelie was in the sitting-room, huddled in an armchair. She had stopped crying but her face was stained with weeping.

Janey went into the kitchen and made two cups of coffee. She gave one to Amelie and sat next to her, cradling her own cup.

For a few minutes they drank in silence. Then Janey spoke.

'You mustn't give in, you know. I knew nothing about antiques when I came here. You are as capable as me. You can learn, too.'

Amelie sipped her coffee.

'Martin doesn't want me,' she whispered.

Janey wondered whether she meant it literally.

'Learn as much as you can and he'll soon find you very useful. I want to do less in the shop. I'm relying on you to take my place.'

Amelie sat thinking.

'Will you help me?'

'Of course I will. I'm going to tell Martin that I intend to order you some dresses like mine. When you have the uniform, you'll feel more confident in the shop.'

Amelie gave her a tremulous smile.

'I should like that.'

'And I suggest that you get a notebook and write down everything new that you learn each day. Then in the evening you can study it. It's hard to remember everything you are told, so write it down.'

They finished their coffees.

'Go and freshen up your make-up,' Janey said, 'then go down to Wilson's and get yourself a notebook. When you come back we'll start your lessons.'

Amelie grabbed her hand and squeezed it.

'Thank you. I don't blame you for anything. Well . . . '

'What is it?'

'Nothing. I just wish that Martin . . . ' She gave Janey a watery smile and went into her bedroom.

Janey went downstairs. Martin was sorting a box of old vinyl records. He had a sulky look on his face.

He's changed, Janey thought. He's become hard and unsympathetic. Or was he always like this and I never noticed? Marriage has brought out the worst in him.

'These dolls are appealing,' she said, taking two old-fashioned dolls from a box. An elderly lady had brought them in for a valuation a few days before and Martin had bought them. 'Oh, dear, this dress has a tear in the back of the skirt. Shall I repair it?'

'Please yourself. Where's Amelie?'

'Gone to Wilson's for a notebook. I'm going to teach her what I know and I've suggested she takes notes.'

'Fat lot of good that will do,' he growled.

'Don't take that attitude! She wants to learn. And by the way, I'm ordering her some striped dresses. She'll feel more the part then.'

He opened his mouth to protest but

changed his mind and just shrugged.

Amelie returned in a happier frame of mind and the two girls settled down to her first lesson. Martin watched from the other side of the shop for a while. He looked as if he was simmering with anger. But at last he went down to the stockroom and stayed there till lunchtime.

Janey decided to leave them together for lunch. She couldn't solve all their problems for them and she needed some air.

She changed into jeans and a sweater, collected an eager Pixie from upstairs and set off for a walk. The air was fresh and she breathed deeply. It was good to get away from the shop for a while.

She decided to take Pixie to the Common for a run. Her usual bench was vacant. She walked Pixie for ten minutes then sank gratefully on to the bench and removed the little dog's lead.

'You have a run,' she said. 'I want to think.'

The Common was deserted and there were no other dogs to annoy her pet. Janey leaned back on the bench and lifted her face to the sun. It was so peaceful.

She began to think about Martin and Amelie. Why had he married her if he didn't love her?

A thought occured which at first she brushed aside as disloyal. Amelie's father was wealthy. Was Martin only interested in Amelie as an heiress?

The idea persisted. It was the only explanation. That he'd taken Amelie away from her family and her country only because she would eventually inherit a large sum of money.

She couldn't believe it of him. Martin, who'd been so kind to her, couldn't treat Amelie like that. Could he?

He was ambitious. He'd often spoken of opening other shops eventually. Marriage to Amelie would help him to fulfil his dreams.

Janey shook her head. The idea was ridiculous.

A voice beside her made her jump.

'Janey, what a lovely surprise.'

Kevin was standing next to the bench looking down at her. He must have walked very quietly. She hadn't heard him approach.

'May I sit down?' He sat without waiting for her reply.

'I'm going back to the shop in a few moments.' Janey began to gather up her bag and scarf and pick up Pixie's lead.

'I'm sure you can stay for a minute or two,' he said. 'I haven't seen you for a while.'

Janey put her bag back on the seat but fastened the scarf round her neck.

'How are the lovebirds?'

'Well, I believe.'

'Fancy old Martin getting married like that. And we all had him down to marry you.' He gave her a sly look.

'Martin and I are friends. Nothing more.'

'If you say so. Anyway, it might have left the field open for me.'

'I don't intend to marry for a long

time,' she said. 'I want to concentrate on my writing first.'

'Your little romances.' He laughed.

Janey ignored him and called to Pixie. As usual the little dog pretended not to hear.

'If you married me you wouldn't need to write. I can keep my wife in style.'

Janey longed to point out he couldn't keep his first wife at all. It was known that his first wife had left him after only one year of marriage.

Janey called Pixie again and this time the little Jack Russell ran up to her and stood quietly while her lead was attached.

Janey stood up.

'I'll be getting back now. Goodbye, Kevin.'

'Aren't you going to give me an answer?'

'An answer to what?'

'My proposal.'

'I didn't hear a proposal,' Janey said.

'It was what I meant. You want it

134

formally. Shall I kneel down?'

Janey sighed.

'Please don't. I've told you my feelings about marriage. I really must go now.'

'I'll walk with you.'

There was no way to be rid of him. They walked to the road and Kevin took her arm. She pulled herself free.

'I'm sorry, I prefer to walk on my own.'

Suddenly he put an arm firmly round her waist.

'Janey, I'm not fooling about. I really meant it. I want to marry you.'

A car came up behind them and slowed down. A window was lowered.

Janey was mortified. It was Ashe! He couldn't fail to see Kevin's arm about her waist. She tried to pull herself free but the arm remained firmly in place.

'I've just called at the shop to see you. They didn't say you were out with anyone.'

'We've just met by chance.'

By the way Kevin was holding her, it

seemed an unlikely story. She managed to free herself from Kevin and stepped nearer to the car.

'Did you want to see me about anything in particular?'

Ashe shook his head and the car began to move slowly forward.

'It can wait. I'll be in touch.' He gave her a salute and was gone.

Janey turned a furious face to Kevin.

'Please don't ever hold on to me like that. Whatever must he have thought?'

'Does it matter what he thought?' Kevin looked sulky. 'What is he to you?'

Janey said nothing but began to walk on with Pixie.

'Don't think you'll have a future with Ashe Corby. Why do you think he hangs about on the fringes of the film world. He likes actresses and models — not unsophisticated writers of romances.'

Janey spun round.

'Go away,' she said clearly. 'Go away and leave me alone. Marry you? You must be mad.' She began to walk quickly down the road towards the shop.

Kevin stood for a moment looking after her then began to walk in the opposite direction, back to his car. There was an unpleasant look on his face.

★　★　★

There was a better atmosphere in the antiques shop in the afternoon. Janey was glad she'd left them alone for a while.

They seemed to have made up their differences and were working quite happily together on a catalogue of Italian glass.

'You'd better measure Amelie for her dress and get the order off,' Martin said as Janey came into the shop.

The two girls smiled at each other and Janey went into the office for a tape measure. She found one in a crowded drawer, but as she was closing the drawer, she spotted the pile of plates Ashe had left and which Martin had promised to get valued.

'Oh, no!' she breathed, moving closer

for a better look. A brass jug had been placed on top of the pile and the top plate had broken in two.

She gazed in horror. What could she say to Ashe? He'd think her so careless. But Martin had promised to take them to the valuer. In fact, she thought he'd already done so.

She walked slowly out of the office and into the shop.

'Ashe's plates. You didn't take them to Mr Driver?'

'There's no hurry. All right, I forgot. I'll take them over tomorrow.'

'One is broken,' Janey said tonelessly.

Martin looked up quickly.

'Broken?'

'Yes, there's a brass jug on top of them and one plate is broken.'

Martin hurried across the shop.

'Show me.' He followed her into the office.

They stood and looked at the pile.

'What if they prove to be valuable?' she whispered.

'How could it have happened?'

Martin ignored her question. 'Could Mrs. Pegg have moved the jug without noticing the plates?'

Mrs Pegg was their new cleaner, usually very careful.

'No-one else comes into the office. And I locked them into the cupboard. Who took them out? How on earth am I going to tell him?'

'I'll have to get them over to Driver and hope to goodness they're not valuable. Tell Ashe we'll buy that one off him and do our best to get a replacement.'

Janey was very quiet for the rest of the afternoon, but her thoughts were racing. What a dreadful day.

Kevin's behaviour had repulsed her and she felt sick to think that Ashe had witnessed it. What must he think of her? She'd told him that she disliked Kevin but he'd seen them with Kevin's arm around her waist.

She flushed again at the memory.

Furiously she rubbed a silver cloth over a Georgian coffee pot. Why had

Ashe called at the shop to see her? Martin hadn't mentioned it and she didn't want to ask him if Ashe had said anything or left a message for her.

She replaced the coffee pot on a shelf and attacked a candlestick. How could she tell Ashe about the plate? He'd trusted them to her and now one was broken.

'Janey, I have made tea.' It was Amelie from the doorway. 'I have some of those macaroons that you like.'

'It hasn't been a very nice day.' Janey removed her protective gloves and replaced the candlestick. 'Did you know that one of Ashe's plates is broken?'

Amelie looked down at the floor.

'No. I know nothing about plates.'

Janey thought she had a rather strange expression on her face but made no comment.

Martin had gone out so the two girls took their break together without him.

'Did you see Ashe at lunchtime when he called at the shop?' Janey asked casually.

The French girl frowned.

'Ashe? No, I don't think he came here. Ah, but of course, I went to the cake shop at lunchtime.'

Janey nodded.

'It's not important. He said that he might call.' She took another macaroon. 'I can't resist these!'

She and Pixie arrived at Pippin Cottage later as Daniel was getting off his bicycle at the gate.

'I've something to show you!' He was excited.

In the kitchen, he hurried to the table and opened his sketchpad. He said nothing but watched as Janey studied the carefully drawn garden design.

Daniel had replaced the simple patio with a large area of asymetrical flagstones. This was broken up by four beds of different types of small trees and shrubs.

Beyond this, he'd kept the lawn but shaped it with an unusual wavy line. Janey traced it with her finger.

'I like this,' she said. 'It's different.'

'The autumn shrubs, acers, azaleas and conifers will give you colour all through the cold weather when there are few flowers. And you can plant bulbs around them for the spring.'

Janey looked at him admiringly.

'You have done your homework, haven't you?'

He flushed but looked pleased.

'Beyond the trees I've made another grassy area,' he said. 'This gap through the shrubs leads up to a small fountain. Would that be all right?' he asked anxiously. 'You'd have to buy one.'

'I think I could manage that,' she said with a smile.

'There's room for a small vegetable garden at the end if you want that,' he said. 'I've put seats at intervals round the garden so that you'll get a different view wherever you sit.'

He sat back, studying the plan, then looked at Janey.

'What do you think?'

He looked so anxious that Janey wanted to hug him.

'I think it's wonderful. It'll look interesting all the year round. Let's go for it.'

Daniel grinned delightedly.

'The next thing is to photograph everything as it is now.' He glanced out of the window. 'Do you think it's too late?'

'Daytime would be better. Any chance you could come over on Sunday?'

Daniel thought.

'Sometimes Dad takes me out on a Sunday, but he's so wrapped up in this filming at the moment, I think I'll be free. Yes, if I can, I'll come on Sunday morning.'

When Daniel was settled at work in the garden, Janey picked up her post. Catalogues, junk mail. Why does no-one do anything about it, she wondered as she shot the offending envelopes into the recycling bin.

But one letter wasn't junk mail. She recognised the address on the back. Her publishers.

She tore it open.

. . . different from your usual work but we liked it very much and should like to offer you . . .

Janey danced round the kitchen waving the letter. Pixie jumped around, too, barking excitedly.

Daniel appeared at the window.

'What's happened?'

Janey waved the letter at him.

'From my publishers. They want to buy my latest book!'

'Good for you!' Daniel waved his rake in the air and returned to his tasks.

Janey looked at Pixie.

'You shall have some of my chicken tonight to celebrate.'

Later, as Janey sat by the fire with Pixie on her lap, she thought over the day. Kevin and a proposal; Ashe and the broken plate; and a new garden design. And her novel had been accepted.

Quite an eventful day.

Mystery At The Ballet

It was no good just worrying about it, Janey told herself as she took her coffee break alone the next morning. She'd have to ring Ashe and tell him about the plate. She couldn't wait for Martin to get them valued.

She was surprised to find Ashe at home. She'd thought he might be up in London. He listened to her faltering explanation in silence, then he chuckled.

'Poor Janey. Have you had a sleepless night over a plate?'

'It's not amusing. You trusted them to me. They might be valuable.'

'I shouldn't think so. They've been in a cupboard for years and nobody has ever mentioned them. They have no distinguishing marks on the bottom.'

'Then why did you bring them to me?' she asked, beginning to feel annoyed.

There was silence for a moment.

'To see you. To get your interest.'

It was Janey's turn to be silent.

'You make me feel rather foolish.'

'Janey, please. I wanted to see you. I thought it was a way to get your attention. Forgive me?'

Janey sighed.

'I forgive you. But I'll still get the plates valued and we'll still pay you for the broken one.'

'I have a better idea,' he said. 'Let me give you the plates as a birthday present. Then you won't have to worry about them.'

'But it's not my birthday.'

'Well, you must have a birthday at some time. Everybody does.'

'We'll have them valued first,' Janey said. 'Now, could I ask you why you called at the shop yesterday?'

'I wanted to invite you to a dinner party. Dr Shepherd and his wife will be there and a few of my archery friends.'

'That would be lovely. At what time?'

'Come at seven-thirty, then we can talk before the others come.'

Janey replaced the phone and stood thinking. A dinner party. What should she wear?

The shop door bell rang. A customer. Clothes would have to wait.

She went into the shop to greet the couple who were looking around.

Ceri was waiting outside when Janey and Pixie left the shop that evening.

'This is a nice surprise,' Janey said. 'Can you come home for a meal?'

'I only have an hour. I wanted to tell you my news.'

Janey studied her friend. She looked as if she was about to explode. An idea flashed into her mind.

'It's not Kyle, is it? He hasn't asked you to marry him?'

Ceri gave a peal of laughter.

'Good gracious, no. What a mad question. He's not the marrying kind, not unless it was to someone who could advance his career. No, it's more important than that.'

They had reached Pippin Cottage and were soon seated comfortably with tea and a lemon drizzle cake in front of them.

'Go on then. Surprise me.'

'I've got a new part in the film,' her friend said. 'A named part and three lines.'

'Wow!' Janey was impressed.

'I'm Lady Cerys and I attend on the queen.'

'Who's playing the queen?'

'We don't know yet. There's a rumour that it's a famous actress but that doesn't sound likely. This is only a small budget film.'

'Have some more cake to celebrate.' Janey offered the plate.

'I daren't. I've been fitted for my costume.'

'Talking about clothes, Ashe has invited me to a dinner party at his house tomorrow. What d'you think I should wear?'

'Aha. So Ashe is getting keen.'

'Don't be silly. It's just a dinner party.'

148

'I'll bet when you get there you'll find it's just the two of you,' Ceri teased.

'Doctor and Mrs Shepherd are going and a few of his archery friends. So, what should I wear?'

Ceri thought.

'What about your navy silk trousers and that white pleated top you bought last month?'

'Good idea. I haven't worn it yet.'

Ceri jumped up.

'Must go. Rehearsal.'

'You do have rehearsals at funny times.'

'Fit them in where we can. Bye. I'll be in touch. I want to hear all about the dinner a deux!'

'It won't be like that. I've told you, there are several other guests.'

Ceri's reply was a loud laugh as she flitted down the garden path and disappeared.

Ashe was waiting on the drive when Janey drove up to Forest Mere. She braked and he opened her door.

'Good. You came early as I asked. It's

a lovely evening; we shall have some drinks in the garden.'

He put an arm round her waist and led her to where a table and some chairs had been placed on the lawn under a tree. Its pale green leaves were edged with white giving it an ethereal look in the early evening light.

'What a beautiful tree. What is it?'

'A box elder. It looks airy-fairy but it can stand really low temperatures. I'm very fond of it.'

Janey sank into a wrought-iron chair with a thick, soft cushion. Ashe poured them each a drink from a cut-glass jug.

'Don't forget I'm driving.'

'This is non-alchoholic.'

Janey tasted the golden liquid.

'Very nice.'

'Like you.' Ashe lifted his glass to her, 'though nice is not a word I should have chosen. Charming is better.'

Janey looked at him over the rim of her glass.

'So, who is coming to dinner apart from Doctor Shepherd and Margaret?'

'Jim, one of my friends from the archery club and his wife, Karen. Jim is an expert archer. He wins medals and takes classes. A real enthusiast.'

'Then why isn't he helping with the film?'

Ashe sipped his drink.

'Not his thing,' he said at last. 'You need to be a bit of a show-off and a bully.'

'Like you,' Janey teased.

'Like me,' he agreed.

'And his wife — Karen?'

'She's a genealogist. You know, family trees. Spends all her life on her computer. Very knowledgeable, I believe.'

'I shan't have anything in common with either of them,' she said after a moment's thought.

'Perhaps Karen will give you some ideas for a book. 'Have you done any historical stories?'

'No, but I intend to.' Janey felt a twinge of guilt when she thought how she'd envisaged him as the villain in her latest work. 'That's an idea. I shall have to discuss it with her. Who else will be there?'

'Gordon and Mike, also from the club. No wives, I'm afraid. They've long gone. And to make up the ladies, Susanne, costume designer for the film and Doctor Julia Fairey from the local practice. Perhaps you know her.'

'She's my doctor, so yes, I know her.'

'Oh, I nearly forgot, my son Daniel will be there, and his cousin Imogen.'

Janey swallowed a mouthful of her drink almost too quickly and nearly choked. Daniel would be there. They'd have to be very careful when they talked.

Ashe looked at her with concern.

'Are you all right?'

'Yes, of course. Just swallowed too quickly. Tell me about Imogen.'

'She's my sister's girl. She and Daniel have always been as thick as thieves, though they're nothing alike. She's very serious and works her socks off at school. Wants to be something big in the business world.'

Before Janey could say anything, cars

began to pull up on the drive. Ashe jumped up, helped her to her feet and they both went to greet the other guests.

Janey was relieved to see that none of the other ladies was too dressed up. She felt comfortable in her outfit and settled down to enjoy herself.

The food was excellent. Mrs. Carlson was an extremely good cook.

'I make no apologies for starting with prawn cocktail,' Ashe announced. 'I know it's very seventies but I love it.'

The main course was roast lamb. Daniel and Imogen helped to bring in dishes of vegetables and clear away plates.

Janey observed the young girl, Imogen. An idea was beginning to form in her mind. Imogen was almost as tall as Daniel with long fair hair tied in a ribbon at the back of her head, She was pretty but not in an obvious way. She wore an ankle-length deep lilac dress and she and Daniel giggled and whispered together as they scuttled in and out of the dining-room.

Daniel, startled to see Janey there, was

almost obvious in his avoidance of her. Janey was worried that Ashe would notice.

She sat between him and Dr Shepherd. Karen sat opposite and Janey was soon able to engage her in conversation about her research.

'Janey is a novelist,' Ashe informed the company. 'I think she had some exciting news recently.'

All eyes turned to Janey who blushed.

'I've heard my publishers want to buy my latest book.'

There was a burst of applause.

'I believe its not easy to get published,' Dr Fairey said.

'It's not my first. That makes it a little easier. The first one is always the problem.'

'Janey's hoping you can give her some ideas for a historical novel,' Ashe said to Karen. 'You know, stories from the past.'

'I'd love to. Perhaps we could meet some time.'

Conversation became general. Janey joined in now and then but mostly she watched the other guests. And Ashe. He looked so handsome in a dinner jacket, she thought. But then, he looked handsome in anything.

She studied him covertly, a little smile playing about her lips.

'May I share the joke?' Dr Shepherd asked quietly.

'Joke? Oh there's no joke. I was just thinking.'

'I can guess what.' Dr Shepherd looked pointedly at Ashe.

Janey gave him a severe look.

'You have too vivid an imagination. Drink your coffee.'

Dr Shepherd gave a chuckle.

'I'm good at matchmaking. Jane Austen can't touch me.'

When the evening ended, Janey was the last to leave. Ashe wound his arm about her waist as the others left and kept her by his side. When they were alone, he walked her to her car.

'We're filming the last of the forest scenes tomorrow,' he said. 'Would you like to come and watch?'

'I'd love to. Same time as before?'

'That's right. Early start, I'm afraid.'

Janey opened the door of her car. Ashe put his arms round her shoulders and pulled him towards her.

'Thank you for coming this evening.'

His other arm skipped around her waist and he bent his head towards her. His lips met hers with a gentle pressure. This was not a fleeting kiss. She lifted her arms and wrapped them around his neck. The pressure of her lips answered his.

He lifted his head.

'The moon is shining in your eyes,' he said. 'My sweet Janey.' He kissed her again.

Reluctantly she forced herself to pull away from him and slid into the driving seat.

'See you in the morning,' he said and closed the door. As she turned at the top of the lane, she glanced in the mirror to see him standing motionless, watching her.

The phone was ringing as she

entered Pippin Cottage. It was Ceri.

'Where have you been? I've been ringing all evening.'

'To the dinner party at Ashe's house.'

'I had forgotten.' Ceri sounded contrite but Janey felt vaguely annoyed that her activities should be so soon forgotten by her best friend.

'What did you want?' Janey scooped up Pixie and held her under one arm. 'Is it anything important, only I've just got in.'

'I'll say it's important. We filmed the castle scene today with the queen and guess who it is?'

'Oh, Ceri, how should I know?'

'Maria Marchant! Stars don't come much bigger and I'm in two scenes with her.'

'Why on earth should Maria Marchant want to be in a little film like yours?'

'She's mad about castles. She's over in England to make a big film but when she heard about this — from your Ashe, I believe — she wanted to have a tiny part in it.'

Janey remembered Ashe saying that Maria Marchant wanted a castle to live in while in England. She hoped he wouldn't see too much of her.

When she arrived at Forest Mere early the next morning there was no sign of Daniel and Imogen but Mrs Carlson greeted her cheerfully and placed a dish of hot croissants in front of her as before.

'I did enjoy dinner last night, Mrs Carlson,' Janey told the housekeeper. 'Where did you learn to cook like that?'

'My mother taught me all I know.'

'That lamb melted in the mouth!'

Ashe came in and took his place at the table after kissing Janey on her forehead. Remembering his kisses of the night before, Janey concentrated on her croissant. He smiled at her as if reading her thoughts but said nothing. 'Shall we be going to a different part of the forest?'

'Oh, yes, we'll move about. I'm glad to see you're well wrapped up. The morning is chilly.'

'Are you fencing today?'

'No, archery. Young Kyle has been practising hard. I hope we'll be able to finish the scenes.'

'You don't film the story in chronological order, do you? It must be hard for the actors.'

'It's how it's done. To film chronologically would take longer and cost more money.'

'Ceri phoned me last night. She was very excited. She said that Maria Marchant had been filming with them.'

Ashe looked up.

'I know she was working on Wynn to let her do the part. Seems she succeeded.'

Janey studied him under her eyelashes. He didn't seem particularly concerned at the mention of the film star.'

'Will she be there today?'

'Shouldn't think so. The queen only comes into the castle part of the story.'

Half an hour later they had loaded the car with bows and quivers full of arrows and the usual mysterious boxes and were bumping their way down the forest tracks. This time Janey was prepared for the scene of chaos which awaited them, quietly found a chair with a good vantage point and allowed Ashe to prepare for the coming scenes. Kyle, the leading man, had already settled himself on the wide spreading branches of an old oak tree not far from her. He waved and she waved back, surprised he remembered her.

Ashe strode up to the tree and spent some time underneath, shouting up instructions to Kyle. Then a coach, pulled by two black horses appeared making its bumpy way along the path which led beneath the tree. Kyle took aim, fired an arrow, jumped lightly from his branch and disappeared into the forest.

The coachman on the front of the coach slumped sideways. Janey wanted to applaud, but something warned her to keep silent. It was as well she did. Ashe appeared with a face like thunder.

'That wretched boy!' He strode away in search of the hapless Kyle.

The scene was set up again. This time Ashe seemed satisfied though Janey could see little difference.

For the rest of the morning, she watched, fascinated, as different scenes were filmed. Sometimes, if it was a difficult scene, Kyle pointed his arrow towards someone or something and Ashe actually made the shot. Janey felt very proud of him.

At last, Wynn, the director called a halt.

'Back again at two sharp,' he said and strode away.

Ashe came to find Janey.

'I'm not needed this afternoon,' he said. 'Shall we go home?'

They climbed into the car and bumped their way along the paths again to the main road.

'Do you like the ballet?'

Janey's eyes shone.

'That's my favourite! But if you don't go to the big cities you get very little

161

chance to see it.'

'There's a small touring company playing at the theatre at Aldersworth. They're Russian so they should be good, would you like to go this evening?'

'I'd love to.'

'I'll be back for you in two hours.'

Impulsively, Janey reached across and kissed his cheek.

'Thank you. That sounds perfect.'

★ ★ ★

The theatre at Aldersworth was an Edwardian gem. It was decorated in red and gold and still boasted two boxes.

The theatre was full. Ashe nodded to two or three people but made no effort to go and speak to them. Janey was flattered to feel that all his attention was devoted to her.

The ballet was 'Swan Lake', a work Janey had seen many times but enjoyed anew every time. The young dancers performed with a fresh enthusiasm which communicated itself to the audience and when the curtain fell at the end of the first act, the applause was deafening.

'Drink, or ice-cream?' Ashe offered.

'Knowing your passion for ice-cream, I'll settle for that.'

'Good.' He grinned. 'We can have a drink afterwards, if you like.'

When he returned to their seats carrying two tubs of ice-cream there was a puzzled look on his face. Janey looked at him enquiringly.

'I'm sure I've just seen Martin and that man you don't like.'

'Kevin Shaw-Coles?'

'That's him. They were standing at the bar.'

'Was Amelie with them?'

'That was the strange thing. There were two young ladies but neither of them was Amelie.'

Janey opened her ice-cream and extracted the spoon.

'I hope you were mistaken.'

'It's possible. I haven't seen either of them many times, but I'm almost sure . . .'

'Did they see you?'

'I don't think so.'

'Well, let's hope we don't bump into them. I don't want to know what's going on. Whatever it is, I blame Kevin. He has the morals of an alley cat. He'd delight in leading Martin astray.'

The ballet began again. Janey tried to concentrate of the stage. Why should Martin spoil her evening. But her mind returned again and again to Amelie. Where was she? Why wasn't she with Martin? Once again she felt sure the marriage was a mistake.

Forcing herself to forget Martin, Janey concentrated on the dancing, admiring the athletic prowess of the Prince and the sharp brilliance of the Swan Queen.

She felt Ashe take her hand and without looking at him, wrapped her fingers around his.

To wild applause, Swan Lake came to an end. As they stood up, Ashe raised his eyebrows.

'Drink?'

'Not here. Let's go before we see those two.'

Ashe hurried her out of the theatre to the car park.

'Where then?' he asked as they fastened their seat belts.

'Would you like to come to Pippin Cottage?' she asked shyly.

He gave her a delighted smile.

'I've always wanted to see inside a dolls'-house.'

Pixie gave them both an ecstatic welcome and honoured Ashe by sitting on his lap while Janey prepared drinks and a snack.

'I'm sorry, I must say it, this is so cute,' he said when she joined him by the fire. 'I feel out of place, like Gulliver.'

Janey place a tray on the little table by the fire.

'Pâte,' she offered. 'I made the toast in a hurry but at least it's not burnt. And I'm afraid I have no red wine. I don't drink it. Men prefer red, don't they?'

'I like white,' he said. He picked up the black bottle in the shape of a cat. 'Black Cat?'

'I brought some back from my cruise on the Moselle last year,' she said. 'It's very pleasant.'

Piixie watched them from her basket, happy to accept Ashe. Perhaps he smells the same as his son, Janey thought.

She was glad the subject of Amelie and Martin didn't come up again. She didn't want to discuss it, or even think about it. There would be time enough for that when she'd been to the shop again and discovered what was going on between the two.

'What made you interested in fencing and archery?' she asked Ashe when they'd finished eating and were lounging back in their armchairs.

'I suppose I liked playing Robin Hood when I was a child, like many small boys. But I became really interested at university. We had an enthusiastic drama group and as well as acting, we hired professionals to teach us stage fighting. I took to it like a duck to water. It really felt natural to me, much more than acting.'

'But you didn't want it as a career?'

'I did, but when the family business needed a firm hand, it fell to me to take over.'

'What else did you do?'

'All sorts of stage combat classes — judo, martial arts, you name it.'

'Have you worked on many films?'

'Not many. I've done some stage work, but really I've been too busy. But I have fight director qualifications if ever I wanted to do more.'

'How do you decide what the actors will do? Or does the director tell you what he wants?'

'You get a vision in your head of how you want a scene to look then you discuss it with the director and the actors. You talk about what motivates them. Rhythm is important. It mustn't be the same tempo all the way through. Think of it as a piece of music.'

She smiled at his enthusiasm.

'It sounds a very interesting hobby.'

'I'm sorry. I tend to go on when I start talking about it.' He stood up.

'Now I really must be going. It's late. Thank you so much for a wonderful evening.'

Janey put her hand on the door to open it but he held her back. Without a word, he took her in his arms.

Janey closed her eyes as his lips found hers. The kiss was long and sweet.

'Goodnight, my darling,' he said, and kissed her again.

An Accident

When Janey looked out of her window she could see two bicycles being walked up her path and round to the side of the cottage. Daniel had brought Imogen with him. Janey was glad to see the girl. It would give her a chance to get to know her. There had been no chance to talk at Ashe's dinner party. She still had an idea at the back of her mind and this would be an opportunity to see whether it might work.

Daniel produced his drawings for the remodelled garden and the three of them pored over them at the kitchen table.

'Isn't he clever?' Imogen said. 'I couldn't begin to do anything like this.'

'Imogen's very practical. She's going to work in London and be something big in the city.'

'Then Prime Minister,' Imogen laughed.

'Why not?' Janey said. 'There's

already been one woman in the job, why not another? Seriously, though, Imogen, is that what you want to do? Go into business?'

'If I can. I'm not as lucky as Daniel. My father doesn't have a business I can join. I have to make my own way.'

'You're the lucky one.' Daniel's voice was gloomy. 'My future is mapped out for me and I have no say in the matter.'

'But this might influence Uncle Ashe.' Imogen gestured towards the drawing. 'I think it's a great idea.'

Ten minutes later they were all in the garden planning Daniel's photographs. He had an expensive camera and seemed quite at ease with it. After a while, Janey left them to return to the cottage and prepare elevenses.

They sat in the garden, eating and drinking and chatting enthusiastically about Daniel's design.

'I love the idea of a gap in the hedge leading to a fountain,' Imogen said.

'Daniel and I will choose it together,' Janey told her. 'He knows what he wants and I know what I can afford.'

Daniel chuckled and took another cake.

'I have a list of the flowers we'll plant. I want masses of colour in patches just here and there near the seats.'

'Scented ones, I hope,' Janey said.

'Definitely scented ones. Roses, lilac, viburnum, honeysuckle.'

'You'll be wasted in the family firm,' Imogen said. 'You must be a garden designer.'

'Tell that to my father,' Daniel replied bitterly, 'or perhaps you'd better not. Just a mention of it brings out the worst in him.'

Janey decided to test her new idea.

'Do you think your uncle would let you go into the family firm?' she asked, turning to Imogen.

The young people looked at her.

'I don't think so,' Imogen said. 'There's really only room for one and that has to be Daniel. Mum and I have discussed it. Uncle Ashe told her he would put in a good word for me with his friends when I've finished college but she seems to think he doesn't see me in a responsible position.'

'I can't interfere,' Janey mused, 'but if he would accept you into the firm, Daniel could go to agricultural college.'

'I'll discuss it with Mum again, but I haven't much hope.'

'I have something to show you,' Janey said to Daniel. 'Wait. I'll get it.'

She hurried into the house. Was she doing the wrong thing? Interfering? She knew the answer but the anguish on Daniel's young face gave her the resolve to continue, whatever the consequence. She took two large envelopes from her desk and returned to the garden.

Daniel looked at them curiously as she handed them to him.

'Open them,' Janey prompted.

Daniel pulled out a brightly coloured brochure from the first envelope. He glanced across at Imogen.

Lawton College of Agriculture and Horticulture.

Imogen moved to sit next to him and

look over his shoulder. Janey watched the two eager faces. Daniel said nothing but pulled another brochure from the second envelope.

'*Worcester Agricultural College*. Janey, did you send for these?'

She nodded.

'I thought you should know what was possible.'

'Uncle Ashe will go into orbit if he sees these,' Imogen remarked.

'He mustn't see them,' Janey said hastily, 'or rather, not until the right moment. Check the qualifications you need to get in,' she said to Daniel, 'so that you'll be prepared, but don't let your father see them yet. We must work on him seeing the possibility of Imogen taking your place first.'

She stood up.

'You two can stay as long as you like, but I must go and get ready to go out this evening.'

'Are you going somewhere nice?'

'A dance at the Village Society. They have one every year. They're usually great fun. Martin is bringing his new wife for the first time. They've fixed me up with a partner — a friend of Martin's. I hope he's nice.'

'Probably Kevin Shaw-Coles,' Daniel said with a wicked grin.

'I think not. Martin knows how I feel about him.'

Daniel and Imogen decided to take Pixie for a walk and left her alone. Janey set out the ironing board and pressed her long, flowered evening dress. She busied herself over her preparations for the evening, trying not to think about Ashe and his reaction if he discovered the brochures before she was ready. She was interferring, she admitted to herself, but who else was there to stand up for Daniel. If he had a mother Janey was sure she would want him to follow his own inclination.

* ★ *

At seven there was a knock at the door. She picked up her bag and stole and hurried downstairs to the door. Martin stood there alone.

'Is Amelie in the car?' Janey asked. 'I thought we could all have a drink here before we set off. I bought some wine especially.'

'Amelie's not coming.' Martin went past her into the cottage. 'She said she didn't feel like it.'

'But I thought she was looking forward to it. And where's the friend you were bringing for me?'

Martin stood in front of her and took her hands in his.

'He's not coming either. It's just you and me. Like in the old days.'

'But . . . '

'Don't keep saying that. It's just you and me. I'm taking you out for a drink before the dance. We don't want to be the first there, do we?'

Janey looked at him in bewilderment. Why had Amelie changed her mind? The last time Janey had spoken of it, Amelie had seemed quite keen on the idea. She had bought a new dress.

Martin picked up her stole and wrapped it round her shoulders. Then he handed her her evening purse.

'Come along. Let's go.'

Janey allowed herself to be swept out of the cottage and down the path. In a few seconds they were in the car and driving quickly down the road.

'We'll go to the Phoenix Hotel,' Martin decided. 'We're rather formally dressed for a village pub.'

Janey didn't answer. She was beginning to feel that the evening was going to be all wrong.

In the Phoenix, a brash, modern hotel that Janey disliked, Martin led her to a seat in a remote corner. He ordered drinks and sat opposite her.

'Nice and quiet. We can talk here,' he said.

'Talk about what?'

The drinks came. Martin emptied half his glass at once as though he needed courage to answer her.

Janey sipped her rose wine and waited.

'We haven't been able to talk like this, on our own, for some time,' Martin began.

Janey said nothing.

'I've missed our talks and our outings,' he went on. 'Marriage has changed things for us.'

'Marriage usually does,' she agreed quietly.

'Have you missed the times we had together?'

'What are you leading up to?' she asked suspiciously. 'Things have changed, yes. I've accepted it. I don't hanker after the past. And there was never anything romantic between us.'

'There might have been. I treated you badly over my marriage,' he said, looking into his glass. 'I admit it. I thought it would be a nice surprise for you. Instead it was a shock. I'm sorry.'

'Must we talk about it? You're married now. I've become fond of Amelie and I think she likes me. Let's leave it at that.'

There was silence for a while.

'I'm not sure that I love Amelie.'

Janey stared straight at him.

'Whatever do you mean?' she asked in a whisper.

'She's been a disppointment. You know my business is very important to me. I thought Amelie, with her background, would add something to it. We'd become a partnership. With her father's connections . . . '

'And his money,' Janey said bitterly.

'There was that, too,' Martin said after a minute. 'But she doesn't seem to take in anything I explain to her. And her memory is dreadful. She's no help at all.'

'Why are you saying this?'

He reached across and took her hand.

'I want things to be the same between us as they used to be. We were close once. I want us to be close again. Amelie need know nothing about it.'

Janey drew her hand from his and stood up.

'It's time we were going to the party.

I shall forget this conversation and I suggest you do so, too.' She marched from the room and he hurried to keep up with her.

Outside, she stopped.

'I'm grateful to you for all you've done for me, Martin, but as we said, things have changed now.' She led the way to the car and they drove in silence to the party.

Inside, all was music, laughter and general excitement. Kevin and a start-lingly platinum blonde were sweeping around in the centre of the room.

They stopped when they saw Martin and came over.

'This is Carole. Janey and Martin,' he said to the girl. He touched Martin's arm. 'We have a table over here. Come and join us.'

Janey sighed as she followed them to a corner table. Carole gave her a weak smile but was obviously more interested in Martin.

'I'll get drinks,' Kevin said, 'then we'll dance.'

Janey danced twice with Martin but conversation was awkward. She had never felt like this with him before. Then, as if to spite her, he made a definite play for Carole. They were both excellent dancers and caused quite a sensation with their Latin-American performance.

Janey returned to her table disgusted with Martin. How could he behave like this when everyone knew he was recently married?

Kevin joined her.

'Don't worry about old Martin,' he said. 'He doesn't mean anything. You know what he's like.'

'I thought I did. Now I'm not so sure.'

'Come along.' Kevin pulled her to her feet. 'Supper.'

'I'm not hungry.'

'You will be when you see the spread. You know how well they do things here.'

Janey allowed herself to be persuaded and discovered that once confronted by the display of party food temptations, she had quite an appetite.

180

'Where's that friend of yours, Ashe Corby?'

'I've no idea. He's not a member of this club, as you know.'

'You could have brought him as a guest. What's wrong? Is the attraction fading?'

Janey ignored this remark.

'I could have brought him,' she agreed, 'but Martin had made other arrangements before I had a chance to ask him.'

'Good. I can have you all to myself.'

Janey looked desperately round the room. How could she get away from him?

Suddenly a club steward rushed into the room.

'Martin Powers,' he called. 'Is Martin Powers here? Phone call.'

Janey looked around. Where was Martin? She'd last seen him dancing with Carole. She rushed back into the room where the band were taking a break and dancing had ceased for the supper interval.

'Is it important? Can I help?'

'It's Dr Shepherd. He said it was urgent.'

'Let me speak to him.' Janey followed the man into the office. She picked up the telephone on the desk.

'Dr Shepherd. It's me — Janey. We can't find Martin anywhere. Is anything wrong?'

'It's Amelie.' Dr Shepherd's voice was serious. 'She's had a fall. I've sent for the ambulance. She'll need to be seen at the A and E. Where on earth is Martin.'

'I'll come. I'll be at the shop as soon as I can.'

She replaced the phone then realised that she had no car. She'd come with Martin. She'd have to get a taxi.

But as she picked up the phone again she had an idea and dialled Ashe's number.

He answered at once. Janey quickly explained the position.

'I'll be with you in ten minutes,' he promised.

Janey retrieved her stole and bag and was waiting outside the entrance when he drove up.

He shushed her thanks.

'Where to? The shop?'

They arrived to find Dr Shepherd supervising Amelie's removal to the hospital. The French girl's eyes were closed and she looked very pale.

'What happened?' Janey demanded.

'Fell downstairs,' Dr Shepherd said. 'I don't understand why she was here. She told Margaret she was going to the party with Martin.'

'He said she changed her mind. I think they must have had a row. Martin was flirting with a girl at the party. I think he may be with her now. We couldn't find him anywhere.'

Dr Shepherd looked disgusted.

'Can you go to the hospital? It would be good for her to see a friendly face when she comes round.'

'Of course,' Ashe said. 'We'll go at once.'

There was no sign of Amelie when

they arrived at the hospital. They sat in the corridor. Janey wrapped her stole around her shoulders and despite the warmth of the building, began to shiver.

'Cold?'

'No. I'm quite warm. I'm worried. Poor Amelie. I wish someone would tell us if she'll be all right.'

'I'll get us some hot chocolate. There's a machine down there. Drinking it will give us something to do.' Ashe disappeared down the corridor.

Janey leaned back in the chair and closed her eyes.

'Excuse me,' a gentle voice said. 'Are you with Mrs Amelie Powers?' A young doctor was standing in front of her.

'Yes. How is she? I'm a friend of the family. Is she all right?'

'She's lost the baby, I'm afraid,' the doctor said. 'A fall downstairs is not good for an expectant mother.'

Ashe had returned carrying two paper cups.

Janey looked at him.

'Amelie was going to have a baby.

Now she's lost it.' Tears began to trickle down her cheeks.

'Can we see her?' Ashe asked. 'I'm a friend. I speak French. It might help.'

'Well, just for a few minutes,' the doctor agreed. 'They're putting her in a side ward now. Do you know how long her husband will be?'

Janey shook her head.

'He's out. We've left a message at his flat.'

The doctor led the way to the little ward where Amelie, now awake but looking frightened, lay in bed, her face as white as the sheets.

'Oh, Amelie.' Janey hurried to the bedside. 'How do you feel?'

Amelie's lip trembled.

'I've lost my baby.'

'We didn't know . . . ' Janey began.

'I only found out today. I thought Martin would be pleased but he wasn't. He shouted at me. He said it was too soon. We couldn't afford a baby yet. The business . . . the business!' She began to cry.

Janey gave an agonised glance towards Ashe. He moved to the chair next to the bed and began gently stroking her arm.

'*Calme-toi, ma petite*,' he murmured. '*Ne parle pas. Reste tranquille.*'

As the soft French words penetrated her mind, Amelie visibly relaxed. The strain in her face began to disappear and she closed her eyes.

Ashe continued to stroke her arm and speak gently. The doctor came in and looked at her.

'She's asleep,' he whispered. 'We've given her something. She should sleep all night.'

He ushered them out into the corridor.

'Come in the morning if you want to,' he said. 'If her husband comes now she'll be asleep and we shan't wake her.'

They thanked him and made their way out of the hospital and into the car park.

'I can't thank you enough for coming with me and for soothing Amelie,' Janey said. 'I think it helped her so much to hear her own language.'

Ashe put an arm round her shoulders and held her very close.

'Shall I take you to the cottage?' he asked, 'or would you like to come back with me for a drink?'

'I think I'd better go to the shop,' Janey decided. 'Martin will return there and will be worried when he can't find Amelie. I'd better be there to explain what's happened to her.'

Ashe looked at her in silence for a few seconds then he nodded.

'Perhaps that would be best. Would you like me to wait with you?'

'Better not.' She gave a faint smile. 'You know what he's like.'

They drove off and were soon at the shop.

'Are you sure you'll be all right?' Ashe looked worried.

'Of course. I'll be fine. I'll phone you tomorrow.'

★　★　★

In the flat, Janey made herself comfortable in an armchair in front of the television. But she couldn't concentrate on a programme and at last she switched it off and made herself a cup of tea.

Her thoughts kept returning to the girl in the hospital bed. Poor Amelie. Away from her home and with a husband who didn't love her.

And to have lost the baby Janey was sure she desperately wanted.

She had just returned to her armchair with her cup of tea when she heard the shop door downstairs being noisily opened.

'Amelie?'

It was Martin's voice. She heard his unsteady footsteps on the stairs.

'Amelie, where are you?'

He stood in the doorway, swaying slightly and blinking at Janey.

'Janey, what are you doing here?'

Janey stood up.

'I hope you've not been driving in that state.'

He ignored the remark.

'What are you doing here? Where's Amelie?'

'You'd better sit down. I'll get you some black coffee.'

She went into the kitchen.

He followed.

'Don't want coffee.'

He turned away and blundered into the bedroom.

'Where's Amelie?' he roared. 'What's happened to her?'

Janey placed a cup of coffee on the little table next to his chair and returned to her armchair.

'Come and sit down and I'll tell you.'

He did as he was told and even took a few swigs of the coffee.

'Amelie's in hospital,' Janey explained. 'She fell downstairs. She lost the baby.'

She watched him as he took in the significance of her words.

'Lost the baby?' he whispered.

Then he jumped up.

'I must go to her. Which hospital is it? Come with me.'

189

'We'll go in the morning,' Janey told him. 'She's sleeping now. They've given her a sedative.'

Martin sat down again and finished his coffee.

'You think I don't love her, don't you?' he said accusingly.

It was what he had said, Janey thought, but she didn't want to antagonise him, so she remained silent.

'I do love her. My little Amelie,' he repeated. 'It's just that my life seems upside-down. I didn't plan to get married yet. It just happened. Now everything's changed. Then she said she was going to have a baby. More changes.'

Janey sipped her tea.

'Well, say something,' Martin said. 'Tell me what you think of me.'

'You need a sleep.'

Janey stood up.

'I'll sleep in the spare room. We'll go to the hospital first thing in the morning when you've had a rest and a shower and feel like talking to people.'

190

Competition

Janey woke early next morning after a night worrying about Amelie and Martin. Surely their marriage couldn't be at an end after such a short time. Martin might be behaving badly at the moment but she was sure that Amelie really loved him.

Ten minutes later a chastened Martin appeared, pale, but dressed and shaved. He was nursing a cup of black coffee but shook his head when she asked if he'd had any breakfast.

'Couldn't eat a thing,' he said.

Janey made herself a cup of coffee and joined him at the table.

He looked uncomfortable.

'Er — about Carole last night,' he began. 'I shouldn't like Amelie to hear of it.'

'Amelie will hear nothing about that incident from me,' she said, 'though from the number of people watching you, there might be someone who would mention it.'

Martin passed a hand over his face.

'I don't know what came over me. We had an argument and . . . '

He looked the picture of misery but Janey was not prepared to indulge him by talking about it.

She finished her coffee and took both their cups into the kitchen.

'Come along. Time to go to the hospital. Shall I drive?'

'Please. I think I'm seeing double.'

Janey wondered what they'd find at the hospital and was relieved to see Amelie dressed and sitting in an easy chair in the dayroom.

'I am so glad you have come early,' she said. 'They have been very kind but I want to go home.'

Martin pulled up a chair next to his wife and wrapped his arms around her.

'Oh, Amelie, how could you fall like that? You might have been killed.'

'But I wasn't.' She looked at Janey

over Martin's shoulder then snuggled close to him.

'I'll go and tell someone we've come for you,' Janey said.

It would be best to leave them alone, she thought.

The formalities of Amelie's release were soon completed and in half an hour they were on their way back to the shop.

'Stop here for a moment,' Martin called to Janey as they approached a flower shop.

He jumped from the car and disappeared but was back almost at once carrying a huge bunch of roses. Amelie, eyes shining, was almost hidden behind the scarlet petals.

'I shan't come in,' Janey told them when they reached Forge Antiques. 'I think you should close for the day so you won't want me. I'll see you tomorrow.'

'Janey, how can I thank you?'

'Don't try,' she said. 'Bye, Amelie. Make sure you rest.'

Janey walked quickly back to the cottage. She'd collect Pixie then spend her unexpected free day working on her manuscript. She had decided to make her heroine an actress and planned to quiz Ceri closely about her time working on the film. She would make a long list of questions to ask her friend.

The phone rang. Martin she supposed. She picked it up.

'Janey, how are you this morning? Did you get any sleep last night?'

'Ashe! Lovely to hear you. Yes, we're back to normal now. Amelie is at home and seems all right. Martin has shut the shop so I have a free day.'

'What a pity. If only I'd known, we could have done something. As it is, I'm just on my way to London. I'm taking young Imogen home on the way.'

'How long will you be gone?'

'A couple of weeks, I'm afraid. I have business to attend to and Wynn wants me to tie up some loose ends about the film. Did you know it was entered for a competition in America?'

'Yes. Ceri said she was going.' Janey was dying to ask if he was going, too, but didn't want to hear the answer. She was afraid it would be yes.

'I'll tell you all about it when I get back from London. Look after yourself.'

Janey replaced the telephone and went back to her desk. Two weeks. London wasn't far away but it might as well be on the other side of the world if she was here and he was there.

She finished the list of questions for Ceri and sat day-dreaming, imagining scenes fron the book, vaguely plotting the story. This was the most enjoyable part of a new book, she decided.

The telephone rang again. She picked up the receiver.

'Janey.' It was Martin.

'Yes? What's happened? Is Amelie all right?'

'She's fine. But I have to go out for an hour. Could you come and be with her? I'm sorry to call you back but I don't want to leave her alone.'

Janey looked regretfully at her desk but spoke brightly.

'Of course I'll come. Is there any hurry? Because if not, Pixie and I will walk.'

'Any time in the next hour. Thanks, Janey, you're an angel.'

In the flat, Amelie was resting with her feet on a stool, working at her embroidery. She patted the seat next to her.

'Come and sit by me. I'm glad Martin has gone out. We can talk.'

Janey looked at her warily. She didn't want to hear any marital secrets. She sat by the other girl and waited.

'I have to make a confession,' Amelie frowned in concentration at her handiwork. 'I did a bad thing.'

'You did a bad thing?' Janey repeated.

'Very bad. I am ashamed.' Amelie selected a skein of red silk. 'But I must tell you. I must confess.' She took a deep breath. 'I broke the plate.'

'The plate. What do you mean?'

'The plates Ashe brought in to be

valued. You were looking after them. I put the copper jug down heavily on them and broke one.'

'I expect it was an accident.'

'No. It was not. I was jealous that Martin thought you were more useful than me. I wanted to upset you.' She gazed down at her hands which had stopped sewing. 'I am ashamed. You have been so kind to me.'

She looked so dejected that Janey reached over and took her hand.

'Amelie, it really doesn't matter. You were upset. These things happen.'

'But it does matter. It was a wicked thing to do. And what if the plates are worth a lot of money?'

'Ashe assures me that they're not.'

As Amelie opened her mouth to protest again, Janey said, 'The important thing is, how do you feel about me now?'

Amelie lifted her head and gave a tremulous smile.

'I love you,' she said simply. 'You are my friend. You are like a sister to me.

You care about me and help me.'

Janey put an arm around the French girl's shoulders and gave her a squeeze.

'Then that's all right. Don't let's say any more about it.'

An awkward silence was averted when Pixie decided she'd been quiet for long enough and jumped up between the two girls.

'Oh, little Pixie, you are so sweet,' Amelie said and removing her embroidery, pulled the little dog on to her lap.

Pixie, deciding that this was a signal for play, jumped down and raced to find a toy.

In the middle of the activity, Martin walked in carrying a large box.

'Have you bought something interesting?'

'Collected something,' he corrected. 'I popped over to see Reg Driver. I wondered whether he'd had time to look at your plates.'

'We were just talking about them,' Janey said.

'I'd hoped to have some good news

for you,' he said, 'to make up for all your help.'

'And?'

'No luck, I'm afraid. He said they were pretty and some collectors would be interested but you'd be lucky to get a hundred pounds for the lot — especially as one is broken.'

Janey was careful not to look at Amelie.

'Ashe said they wouldn't be valuable,' she said cheerfully, 'so I'm not too disappointed.'

She grabbed Pixie and attached the lead to her collar.

'Come along. Time to go home. See you both tomorrow.'

They were almost at Pippin Cottage when Daniel caught up with them.

'Imogen's gone,' he said. 'Dad took her.'

'I know. He told me when he phoned.'

'I've brought something exciting to show you,' he said.

'What is it?'

'Wait till we get inside,' Daniel seemed to be bottling up his great news with difficulty.

Janey thought he would explode if he didn't tell her soon. She hurried him into the cottage.

'Now. What is it?'

He took a magazine from his school bag and sat at the table.

'Come and see this.'

Janey joined him and looked at the cover of the magazine. *Gardening For All.*

'I believe that's a good magazine,' she commented 'It's certainly very popular.'

Daniel opened it at the centre pages and spread them out. *Enter Our Exciting Competition*, the headline blazed.

Janey looked at him.

'Read it.'

To win our most exciting prize, she read, *show us that you have the skill and artistic ability to convert an ordinary garden into a place of charm and beauty.* She looked at the boy.

'You're going to enter? You're going

to use my garden?'

He nodded enthusiastically.

'Oh, Daniel, do you think . . . ?'

'I've done half the work already,' he said. 'You have to provide before and after photographs. I've got plenty of before ones.'

'But is there time to get everything in place and growing? When is the closing date?'

'In three weeks.'

'Three weeks.'

'It's not a very recent magazine,' he admitted. 'The competition has been running for a while. There's just three weeks left.'

She looked at him in despair.

'Daniel, that's not really long enough.'

'It is. Look at the Chelsea Flower Show. They achieve marvellous results in a very short time. I'll work really hard. I'm sure I can do it. Dad's away for the next two weeks. That will help. He won't know what I'm doing.'

Ashe! How could she have forgotten him? What if the impossible happened and Daniel won the competition?

'You didn't read the prize.' Daniel's face was red with excitement. 'The first prize will be the sponsorship of the gardener at an agricultural college of his or her choice for two years. Can you believe it?'

'But your father?' Janey knew she was pouring cold water on his excitement, but she had to bring him down to earth.

Daniel stuck out his bottom lip mulishly.

'That's not going to stop me. I'll deal with that when I win.'

When you win! Janey thought. Well, she'd encouraged him so far, she couldn't give up now.

She went into the kitchen and prepared a bowl of food for Pixie. Then she picked up her car keys.

'Come along.'

'Where are we going?'

'To get your water feature. In case there's a delay in delivery, we'd better get it ordered.'

'Do you mean it? Oh, Janey, you're wonderful.'

Daniel followed her out to the car almost dancing in his excitement.

At the garden centre, they made their way to the section dealing with water features. Daniel began to study them carefully. Then he looked at Janey.

'I forgot to ask. How much can we spend?'

'Let's choose one first then I'll see whether I can afford it.'

'I don't want a big one but it must be as tall as possible,' he muttered.

Luckily the garden centre was large and had a good selection. There were barrels being filled by taps; imitation trees with squirrels on the branches; silver balls shining as water cascaded over them and even a wall of water.

'I love the old-fashioned fountains, but they're too big,' the boy said. 'What about this?'

From the centre of a small pool, a nymph stood on tiptoe, reaching up with her cupped hands from which water bubbled down over her body.

Janey and Daniel looked at each other.

'It's perfect.' Then she saw the price. It was fifty pounds, more than she'd expected to pay. She looked at Daniel. How could she tell him it was too expensive?

Mentally she reviewed her last bank statement. She could just manage if she forgot about the new coat she'd intended to buy. What was a coat compared to a beautiful fountain. She realised that Daniel was looking at her hopefully.

'It's rather expensive, isn't it?'

Janey put an arm round him

'Not at all. Come along. Let's go and order it.'

'Can we come for the plants in a day or two?' Daniel asked as they drove back to the cottage.

Plants! Janey had forgotten them. That would mean more expense.

'I'm taking all my money out of my money box,' Daniel told her. 'I was saving for a camcorder but this is more important. I can't take any out of my bank savings account — Dad keeps that — but my money box is different.'

'How much have you got?'

'Twenty five pounds. Will that be enough?'

'It's my garden, I'll pay for the plants.'

'You've paid for the fountain, I'll buy the flowers,' Daniel said, 'but you can help if I haven't got enough.'

They drove on in silence. Then Daniel spoke.

'My two best friends, Spike and Toby, want to help. Would you mind?'

'I think it's a good idea. You'll find it almost impossible to do on your own. Are they keen gardeners, too?'

'No, but they'll do as I say.'

Janey smiled.

'You'll have to swear them to secrecy.'

They'd reached Pippin Cottage.

'You'd better get off straight away. Mrs Carlson will wonder where you are. See you tomorrow.'

After a simple supper of an omelette and a fruit salad, Janey went to her desk. But she couldn't concentrate.

If only she could tell Ashe what had been going on in her garden. A simple idea, to allow Daniel to indulge his love of gardening, had snowballed into a nationwide competition. What if Daniel won? She hoped he would win, but if he did . . .

It was no good. She could not concentrate on writing. Agatha Christie used to say she worked out her plots while doing mundane things like washing the dishes. Janey went into the kitchen. Ironing! Can't get more mundane than that.

But by the time she had finished ironing she was no further with her plot and her mind was still full of Ashe.

Perhaps she should explain everything to him before it went any further, she thought as she emptied the iron. But how would that affect Daniel? It would break his heart if Ashe forbade him to enter the competition.

She returned to the sitting-room, threw herself on to the couch and pressed the television remote.

'Now our new programme, Gardening Quiz,' the announcer said.

Janey gave a squeal of annoyance.

'Can't I get away from gardens?' she muttered through clenched teeth.

She switched off the television. She would have an early night, she decided. She had a new library book, a nice, juicy murder, the librarian had called it. That would take her mind off gardening.

Her foot was on the bottom stair when the phone rang. She wondered whether to ignore it, pretend she was out, but the caller might be Amelie.

'Hello?' she said into the receiver.

'Janey. I'm not too late, am I? You're not in bed?'

'Ashe. No, of course not. Where are you? London, I suppose.'

'Mm. Wish I wasn't. I'd like to be at home with you.''

'Did Imogen get home all right?'

'Yes. I've been at my sister's house this evening. They invited me to dinner.'

'She's a lovely girl.'

'She is, and so bright. We had a good chat all the way home. You know, she's very intelligent, for a young girl. Good range of knowledge about politics and commerce. I was really surprised.'

Janey glared at the phone. Why shouldn't a young girl be knowledgeable about politics and commerce?

But she didn't want to start an argument.

'Yes. I believe she wants a career in the city.'

There was silence for a few moments. Janey waited.

'Well, I'll have to see what I can do to help,' Ashe said. 'Now, tell me what you've been doing.'

That was the last thing she wanted to do, so she quickly changed the subject.

'Any news about the America trip?'

Ashe was easily diverted to talk about that and it was another ten minutes before they said goodnight.

The Film Star

Amelie had sunk into a depression. There seemed no way to cheer her up. Martin planned outings and surprises for her but she remained quiet and withdrawn.

At last, Janey had an idea.

'Why don't you take her to France for a holiday? I can manage very well, as you know.'

Martin looked at her.

'Janey, you're a wonder. Why didn't I think of that. Let's go and tell her.'

'No. You go and tell her.'

He gazed at her for a moment then bent and kissed her forehead before racing upstairs, two at a time.

Janey stood looking after him. Why couldn't men see the obvious, she wondered.

Martin and Amelie left the next day, Amelie's face bright and smiling.

Janey waved goodbye and went back into the shop. Once again she was in charge of Forge Antiques. She hoped their return wouldn't bring a surprise like last time.

Business was quiet. Janey spent the morning polishing and rearranging her collection of costume jewellery. She'd recently bought several interesting pieces from a house clearance sale: a silver bracelet set with turquoises, a dainty filigree necklace and her favourite, a bracelet of oval and round rose-cut garnets.

She picked up the bracelet and wrapped it round her wrist. Beautiful, Deep wine-red stones. Perhaps she'd save up and buy it for herself. Then she remembered the fountain and flowers for her garden and replaced the bracelet. It would be some time before she could splash out money on a bracelet.

She had just locked the display cabinet and picked up a soft duster when the shop door bell rang. She walked towards it.

Kevin Shaw-Coles sauntered in looking very pleased wih himself. He had a newspaper under his arm. He looked round the shop.

'Not very busy, I see.'

Janey was instantly on the defensive.

'We are usually busier in the afternoon,' she said. 'People often go for a drive and pop into shops like this.'

He held up his hands.

'You don't have to make excuses to me. It was only an observation. How about a cup of coffee?'

'I can't leave the shop.'

'You could make me one here. I've brought something to show you.'

She moved towards the office.

'Very well. I'll make some.'

Kevin followed her and took a seat at the desk.

'When will the newly-weds return?'

'In a week, I expect. Unless they intend to stay longer.' Janey poured the coffee into two cups and handed one to Kevin.

'Thank you. Now come and sit down

and I'll show you something interest-ing.'

He unfolded the newspaper and spread it out on the desk. In the centre of the page was a large photograph. Janey looked closer. Ashe was walking with an elegant Maria Marchant. She was smiling up into his face and he seemed to be holding her arm.

Janey looked at Kevin.

'Read the headline,' he said.

MARIA'S LATEST SQUEEZE. WHO IS THE NEW MYSTERY MAN?

He smiled.

'We know, don't we? Ashe Corby, who is pretending to be interested in you.'

Janey felt her face flush.

'They're working on the film together,' she said. 'That's why he's in London, tying up loose ends with Wynn, the pro-ducer.'

Kevin gave a bark of unpleasant laughter and began to fold up the newspaper.

'Would you like it?' he asked. 'Perhaps Ashe hasn't seen it. You should show him when he comes back.'

'No, thank you.' Janey's voice was icy. 'I'm sure he'll tell me all about it. If you've finished your coffee, I'll wash the cups and carry on with my work.'

'You want me to go?'

'You've done what you came to do — show me the photograph, so, yes, I'd like you to go.'

He got up reluctantly.

'Very well, but I'll leave it anyway. It's of no interest to me.'

At the door he hesitated.

'Dinner tomorrow night?'

'I'm busy.'

'And every other night, I expect.'

Janey made no answer.

Kevin gave a little wave of his hand.

'Bye, Janey. See you.'

As soon as he was out of sight, Janey locked the door and put the *CLOSED* notice up. It was lunchtime anyway. She went back to the office and unfolded the newspaper again.

For a long time she gazed at the photograph.

She had never believed Ashe could be interested in someone as unsophisticated as her. She was just a novelty to amuse him while he was in the country. Maria Marchant was a much more suitable love interest. She bit her lip as tears began to fill her eyes.

Despite what she'd said to Kevin, business was quiet that afternoon. She had two customers but they only browsed and her till remained empty. At four o'clock, she closed the shop, changed out of her striped dress and took Pixie for a long walk through the woods.

They followed the path to the butts and Janey was pleased to see Jim, Ashe's friend, carrying rubbish from the hut to his car.

'Hi,' he called. 'Nice to see you.'

'You're working hard. What's this? Spring cleaning?'

'Someone has to do it,' he replied. 'The hut's a real mess. Can I make you a drink. I was just going to have one.'

Janey remembered the catering

arrangements in the hut but forced herself to say, 'That would be nice.'

She and Jim sat with their mugs on a fallen log. Janey looked around.

'Doesn't the forest look beautiful?'

'Aye, it does that,' he agreed. 'Have you heard from Ashe?'

'Just phone calls. He seems very busy.' She couldn't resist asking, 'Did you see his photo in the Daily News?'

'With the American glamour girl?' He gave her a sharp glance. 'You didn't take any notice of that, did you?'

Janey flushed.

'Of course not. Newspapers are always looking for a story.'

They sat in silence for a few minutes then Jim said, 'How'd you like an archery lesson? It would be a surprise for Ashe when he gets back.'

Janey smiled.

'What a good idea. Have you time?'

'Of course. I'm fed up of housework anyway.'

They caught Pixie, who was having a lovely time in and out of the hut, and tied her, protesting, to a tree, well away from danger. Jim collested a few bows while Janey took off her coat.

'Now we'll have to see which one suits you,' he said.

He checked the length of the bow and the arrows. He made her cover each eye in turn to see which was the dominant one and he tested her strength as she pulled back the string.

'Now let's get your stance right.'

'You're a real slave driver,' Janey protested. 'When can I shoot an arrow?'

'In one minute. There's a few safety rules you must remember first. Always carry your arrows behind you in case you fall. And approach the target from the side, also in case you fall on an arrow.'

'Now can I shoot an arrow?'

For the next hour Janey had a wonderful time. It wasn't easy. The string felt slippy, the bow was awkward and the arrow kept sliding off and falling to the ground. But she persevered.

'Everyone thinks it's easy till they

try,' Jim said. 'But you're doing very well for a beginner.'

'Do you think I'll ever make an archer?' she asked.

'We'll have a few more sessions then you can give Ashe a demonstration. I think he'll be pleasantly surprised.'

On the way home, she called in to see Margaret and Dr Shepherd. The doctor was out but Margaret was pleased to have a visitor. She gave Pixie a drink of water and let her out into the garden, then she and Janey settled down to a nice gossip. Janey told her what she'd been doing that afternoon.

'That was kind of Jim. I'm sure Ashe will be pleased.'

'He won't be impressed by my skill at the moment,' Janey said, 'but Jim has promised me another lesson so I might improve after that.'

'Have you heard from Martin and Amelie? They're in France, aren't they?'

'Nothing so far. I hope they're too wrapped up in each other to think of me.'

Margaret thought for a moment.

'Will Amelie ever be what Martin wants in the antique business?'

'It's not what she wants. She wants to work with children.'

'Is she qualified?'

'She was doing a college course in France. I don't think she'd finished it when she got married and left the country.'

'Couldn't she go to college here?'

'She could, but I think it would be best if she could get some sort of job in a nursery or creche until she settles down.'

There was a whistle from outside the door and Dr Shepherd came into the room.

'Janey!' He gave a wide smile when he saw her. 'This is a nice surprise. Any tea in the pot?' he asked, giving Margaret a kiss.

'I'll make some fresh.' Margaret bustled out of the room.'

'Well, how are things? You're in charge again, I hear.' The doctor reached out and took two cakes. 'These are only a mouthful each.'

'We were talking about Amelie. She wants to work with children, not antiques.'

Margaret came back into the room with the teapot.

'You're well in with the people at Little Bears Nursery,' she said to her husband. 'Might they have a vacancy for an assistant?'

Dr Shepherd considered.

'I could ask them.'

'That would be wonderful,' Janey said. 'Even a part-time position would help.'

'What about Martin?' the doctor asked. 'Would he object?'

'I think he had such a shock over Amelie's fall, he would agree to anything,' Janey said.

'More tea?' Margaret asked after a while.

Janey stood up.

'No, thank you. We'd better be getting home.' She almost said, 'I must see what the boys have been up to,' but stopped herself just in time. The fewer people who knew about the garden project the better.

At Pippin Cottage, the three boys were packing up. They refused refreshments but insisted on Janey inspecting their work. She was most impressed. Paths had been neatened and edged, benches were scrubbed and flower-beds prepared for the plants.

'Could we go to the garden centre tomorrow?' Daniel asked hopefully, 'or will you be too busy?'

'Of course. Are we all going?'

The others nodded enthusiastically.

'Right,' Janey agreed. 'As soon as I get back tomorrow, we'll go.'

When they'd gone home, she took another look around the garden. It was difficult to believe they'd done so much in such a short time.

Ashe phoned that evening. After a short discussion on what they'd each done since the last call, he said suddenly, 'I'm missing you a lot. Have you missed me?'

Janey found it hard to answer immediately. Of course she missed him, but the newspaper photograph kept dancing before her eyes.

'Why do you hesitate?' he asked. The laugh that accompanied the question was forced. 'Don't you miss me even a little bit?'

'Of course I do, it's just that . . . well, I saw the photograph in the Daily News.'

This time he gave a loud laugh.

'The one with Maria and me?'

'Yes,' she replied in a quiet voice.

'If the photograph had been larger, it would have included Maria's fiancé. But of course that wouldn't have made such a good story. Janey, my love, you know me. Maria is a sweetie, but not my type.'

'She's very glamorous.'

'She is, and very high-maintenance. And very self-centred. My type is quite different. I think you know what I mean.'

'Oh, Ashe.'

'I'm rather partial to gentle little romantic novelists who live in tiny cottages in quiet villages.'

'Oh, Ashe,' she said again. 'I really do miss you.'

'I'll be back soon. Till then, goodnight, my darling.'

'Marry Me!'

Martin and Amelie returned from France in a very happy mood.

'It was so lovely to see my family,' Amelie told Janey. 'They were so sorry about my accident. Of course I didn't tell them about the baby.'

She handed Janey a little parcel. Janey opened it to find small tablets of soap in an earthenware dish. Across the top were laid sprigs of lavander.

'Special lavender soap, made in Provence. I think you will like it.'

Martin returned from carrying cases into the bedroom.

'Splendid news about Kevin, isn't it?'

Janey looked at him blankly.

'Hasn't he told you? Well, I can't say anything. He'll be round to tell you himself, I'm sure. The lucky devil.' He went downstairs to bring in more bags from the car, chuckling to himself.

The telephone rang. It was the garden centre. The fountain would be delivered that afternoon. Janey said she would be there.

Just before lunch, Dr Shepherd appeared. He gave a little nod and a smile to Janey. She guessed that meant he had some good news. She took him upstairs and beckoned to Amelie to follow.

'I don't know whether Janey has told you . . . ' he began.

Janey shook her head.

'There hasn't been time.'

'I believe you'd like to work with small children,' he said. 'You were at a training college in France?'

'Yes, but I didn't finish my course. But yes, that is what I'd like most of all.'

'A young lady whom I know very well runs the Little Bears Nursery. She has a vacancy for an assistant. I mentioned you to her and she would like you to call and see her if you are interested.'

'Oh, yes, I am so interested!' Amelie

pressed her hands together. 'I should like that so much. When can I go to see her?'

'She said that tomorrow, when the nursery closes, would be very convenient. Perhaps Janey will go with you.'

When he left, Martin came up from the cellar.

'What did Doctor Shepherd want? Was it a check-up?'

'No.' Amelie looked nervously at Janey. 'He came to see me about a position in a nursery.'

There was silence for a moment then Martin said, 'For you?'

'There's a vacancy at Little Bears Nursery,' Janey told him. 'Amelie wants to work with children. We are going to see the owner tomorrow.' She looked at Martin, daring him to object.

Various emotions crossed Martin's face, then he said, 'Right. That sounds very suitable for Amelie. More suitable than antiques.'

Amelie flung her arms round his neck.

'You don't mind, Martin. I am so happy.'

Martin smiled at Janey over Amelie's head.

He was thinking that everything would be as it was before, Janey thought, which was what he wanted. And it tied her more closely to the shop, which was not what she wanted.

She left early to supervise the installation of the fountain in her garden. Luckily it was not as heavy as it looked and the two muscular young men from the garden centre soon had it in place, and water gushing from the top. Janey was fascinated with it and couldn't wait to show Daniel.

When Daniel and Toby arrived, she made them put their hands over their eyes and led them to the top of the garden.

'Now, open your eyes,' she commanded.

There were whoops of delight as the boys did a dance round the nymph in her watery bowl.

'Wait till old Spike sees this,' Daniel said. 'He couldn't come tonight, his mum wanted him at home. He was mad.'

'Come on now,' Janey ordered. 'Let's go and get the plants.'

Daniel produced a long list.

'I hope they have all these,' he said with a frown, 'otherwise . . . '

'Worry about that when they haven't,' she advised. 'I'm sure we'll get most of them.'

An hour later they returned to the cottage laden with plants of every colour and size.

Toby was as excited as Daniel.

'Can we start planting them tonight?' he asked eagerly.

'No. Just spread the trays on the patio and water them. Then they'll be ready to put in the ground tomorrow.'

She felt too tired for gardening and wanted to continue with her novel.

'Doesn't your mum wonder where you go each evening?' she asked Toby.

'I've told her I'm helping Daniel with a special project,' he replied. 'She's not very interested as long as I'm not home late.'

'Toby has three-year-old twin sisters,' Daniel said, looking at his friend with sympathy. 'His mum is very busy with them.'

When they'd gone, Janey settled down at her desk with her manuscript. She'd made Ashe the hero, but in her mind's eye she saw him as a very picturesque villain, twirling his moustaches and slapping his riding boots with his whip. But what if he recognised himself? No, it was safer to make him the hero.

She wrote steadily for two hours, then easing her shoulders, she went into the kitchen to make herself a meal.

Ashe rang rather late.

'Sorry, we've been really busy today,' he said.

'With the film?'

'Yes. Wynn's convinced we'll win the American competition.'

'What do you think?'

'I'm not sure. It's very colourful, lots

of action and beautiful girls. But we'll have competion from all over the world. We'll have to wait and see.'

'I'm longing to see the finished version,' she said. 'Ceri seems very pleased, too.'

'Your little friend. Yes, she's done extremely well and looks gorgeous. Wynn has his eye on her for future work.'

'Really? She'll be so pleased.'

'Don't say anything. Let Wynn tell her. Anyway, that's enough about other people. How are you?'

'I'm fine. Martin is back so the responsibility for the shop is off my shoulders again.' She sighed. 'I do wish you were coming home soon.'

'So you do miss me? I'm glad. I miss you dreadfully. But I might have a surprise for you soon.'

'A surprise? Not a surprise like Martin's, I hope.'

'If I told you it wouldn't be a surprise,' he said with a laugh. 'And, no, it's nothing like Martin's. Now I must go. Goodnight, my darling.' He blew her a kiss and replaced the phone.

Janey wandered slowly upstairs. A surprise. What could it be? She was slightly suspicious of surprises now.

The next afternoon, she and Amelie presented themselves at the Little Bears Nursery. The owner and headmistress, Susie Blakemore, was friendly and welcoming. Janey didn't know what Dr Shepherd had said about Amelie but Susie seemed happy to offer her the position once the background checks were done.

They wandered around, looking at the tiny chairs and tables, the plentiful supply of toys, the shelves of books and the interesting outside area with its prams and bikes.

'We have seventy children each day,' she explained to Amelie. 'They are divided into groups. You would help the teacher of the blue group.'

Janey glanced at Amelie. The French girl looked happy and relaxed.

'I'll go and wait in the car,' she told

Susie. 'You two can talk more freely without me.'

She climbed into the car and sat with a newspaper propped up on the steering wheel.

Glancing up she saw a familiar figure coming towards her. She lifted the paper higher but it was too late. She had been spotted.

'I thought I recognised your car,' Kevin said. 'What are you doing here?'

'Waiting for Amelie.'

He wasn't interested in Amelie but opened the passenger door and slid into the seat beside her.

'Did Martin tell you I had some good news?'

'He did mention something.'

'I'll bet he did. He's as jealous as anything. I bet you'll be thrilled.'

'If something nice has happened, I'm pleased for you,' Janey said, 'but I can't believe it affects me.'

'Let me take you out to dinner tonight and I'll tell you how if affects you.'

Janet looked at him. She didn't want to go out to dinner with him and she was sure Ashe wouldn't be pleased if she did.

'Can't you tell me now?'

'It's much too important for that.'

Janey looked out of the window. What a nuisance the man was. Then she had an idea.

'I'll come to lunch with you tomorrow,' she suggested. Lunch was less of a commitment than dinner.

'Well.' Kevin wasn't pleased but accepted the idea, 'Lunch will do, I suppose. I'll pick you up at the shop at one-thirty. Here's Amelie. I'll go.' He waved to Amelie and continued his swagger down the road.

They drove home, Amelie full of animated chatter about her new position, Janey quiet, wondering what Kevin's good news could have to do with her.

Kevin appeared at the shop at twelve-thirty. He and Martin spent their time making silly jokes and slapping each other on the back. Janey had the feeling that she was the subject of some of this jocularity, but wouldn't give them the satisfaction of showing any interest in their behaviour.

Janey looked at Kevin as he started the car.

'Don't let's go too far,' she said. 'I don't want to be late back, whatever Martin says.'

They drove to a small inn in the next village.

'I like it here,' she said. 'I've been several times with Martin.'

'It'll do,' Kevin said dismissively, 'if you don't want to go far.'

Wooden partitions divided the main bar into private areas and Kevin led Janey to the farthest comer. She was glad there was a window next to their table. It made her feel less shut away with Kevin.

'Eat first or news first?' Kevin gave her a smug smile. He seemed to be hugging hiself as if he was going to surprise her with the one thing she wanted to hear.

'Eat, I think.' Janey felt she could face whatever he had to say better on a full stomach.

They both chose gammon and mushrooms and while they were waiting for the food, Kevin asked about Amelie.

'Eventually she'll take over from you, I expect,' he said. 'Then you won't be needed at the shop.'

'She's not really interested in antiques,' Janey said.

'She says that because she feels inadequate beside you. She'll learn.'

'She has a new job. Nothing to do with antiques.'

Kevin stared at her.

'Nothing to do with antiques? But what about the business? Martin is relying on her to help him build it up.'

'Amelie has accepted a position as an assistant at the Little Bears nursery.'

'Plants?'

Janey laughed.

'Children. Little children.'

'But . . .'

'She was studying to be a nursery

234

teacher in France,' Janey said. 'It's all she wants to do.'

'But her father owns several antique shops.'

'That doesn't mean she has to be interested.'

'So Martin will still be relying on you.'

'I'm not looking too far into the future,' she said. 'I'm hoping my writing will be the biggest part of my life.'

'We'll see,' he said mysteriously.

The food arrived and conversation came to an end for a while. But as coffee was brought to their table, Janey realised she could put off the purpose of their lunch no longer.

Kevin put his arms on the table and leaned forward.

'Have I ever told you about my Uncle Angus in Scotland?'

Janey blinked. What could this have to do with her?

'I don't think so.'

'Actually, he's my great-uncle and very wealthy.' He reached into an inside pocket and brought out a photograph. 'He has a huge estate. This is his house.' He handed the photograph to Janey. 'Actually I've never met him, never been to Scotland.'

Janey studied the gothic castle-like house with its towers at each corners and massive studded front door.

'Goodness,' she exclaimed.

He seemed well satisfied with her response.

'Would you like to live there?' he asked.

'Me? Well, it would be a bit different from Pippin Cottage.'

'Marry me and that will be your home.'

Janey stared at him.

'Are you moving to Scotland to live with your uncle?'

'No. Alexander House is mine now. Uncle Angus died last month. He's left everything to me — house, estate and money.' He reached across the table for her hand.

'Marry me, Janey,' he said again.

'We'll have a wonderful life together. You'll want for nothing.'

'But I can't move to Scotland just like that, leave my home and my friends.'

'People move all the time, often much further away than Scotland. Martin thinks it a wonderful idea. He's all for it.'

'But . . . but I don't love you.'

'I think you'd come to love me,' he assured her with confidence. 'I'd do everything to make you happy. And I do love you.'

Janey looked at his earnest face. He was the sort of man who'd never take no for an answer. Suddenly she had to get away. She looked at her wrist watch.

'Oh, dear, look at the time. We must go.'

He grabbed her hand again.

'Promise me you'll think about it.'

'Of course. Yes. I'll think about it.' He released her hand and she hurried towards the door.

Back at the shop, Martin looked at

her enquiringly. Kevin had left her at the door. She ignored Martin and went through to the office to change her dress.

Martin was obviously desperate to know what answer she'd given Kevin but she refused to satisfy his curiosity.

'I'm going to do these VAT forms,' she called and closed the office door.

* * *

That weekend, Daniel and his friends worked hard to produce a set of photographs to do justice to the new garden. They were mounted artistically in a large album — before pictures, then the after ones. Janey told them she was most impressed. She helped Daniel complete the entry form and wrap up the album. Then they took Pixie for a walk to the post office.

'Of course, I shan't win,' Daniel said, 'but what if I did?'

'You mean about your father?'

'Mm. Would he be more mad if I told

him now or if he found out later?'

Janey thought for a while. Ashe would certainly be furious and not only with Daniel.

They had reached the Common and sat on a seat while Pixie raced around.

'Perhaps it would be best to tell him as soon as he gets back. Prepare him. Perhaps he won't mind too much when he sees what you've achieved,' she said hopefully.

Daniel made no comment but jumped up and began to chase Pixie. How nice to be young and able to put worries out of your mind just like that

She had two things to worry about; Ashe and the garden and Kevin's proposal, and neither would leave her mind.

Daniel arrived as usual the next morning. Janey had begun to wonder whether he would come now that the garden was finished.

'I'm going to tidy the tool shed,' he said. 'It's a bit of a muddle after all we've been doing lately.'

Pixie went with him. There was always the chance of a game when Daniel was around.

Janey began to prepare her evening meal.

Suddenly there was a knock at the front door. She dried her hands and went to open it. Ashe stood there, a smile on his face and a large bouquet of roses in his arms.

'Surprise! I've come back early. I couldn't wait to see you.' He presented her with the flowers.

Delightedly she pulled him inside. He took the bouquet from her and put it on a table. Then he took her in his arms.

'This is the best possible surprise,' she said.

Then there was no need for words. Their lips met and Janey was transported on wings of love.

Darling Ashe. He was back and they were together. How could Kevin ever compete with her beloved Ashe?

'I'm making a meal,' she said at last.

'Can you stay or would you rather go out for something?'

'I've been eating restaurant food for days,' he said. 'I just want some home cooking — and you.'

He followed her into the kitchen. She returned to her job of preparing a chicken casserole. He stood behind her and wrapped his arms round her waist. They were standing in front of the window. As he raised his head, he looked out of the window.

'You've made some changes in the garden, haven't you?'

Janey's face flushed.

'Yes,' she said, confused. 'Quite a few changes.'

'Looks good from here,' he said. 'Can we go and see what you've done?'

With a sense of impending drama, Janey followed him into the garden.

'I like it,' he said. 'It's very artistic. Was it your idea or did you have a garden designer?'

'Yes, I did get a garden designer,' she said slowly.

As she spoke, Daniel stepped out of the garden shed. He paused as he saw his father.

Ashe looked from one to the other.

'If it wasn't such a ludicrous suggestion, I'd ask if this was your garden designer.'

'Actually,' Janey began, when Daniel interrupted.

'Yes. I designed the garden. And I worked on it. It's for a competition and I intend to win.'

Ashe stared at his son without speaking.

'And when have you done this?' he asked at last.

'After school and at weekends. You've been out or away so much you haven't noticed where I was.' His voice had a bitter edge to it.

He turned to Janey.

'And you've encouraged this? Well, of course you have. Yet you knew I didn't want Daniel to take up a gardening career. I want him to join me in the family business. How dare you interfere in my plans for my son's future?'

'Your plans? What about Daniel's plans? He has plans for his future, too.'

'Daniel's a child. He doesn't know what he wants!'

'You're wrong there,' Janey said furiously. 'He has very clear plans about what he wants, but you won't listen.'

He turned away from her and stared at his son.

Daniel stared back defiantly.

'Daniel will go into the firm as I did. One day he'll be in charge. He'll thank me then.'

Without a word, Daniel ran down the path and around the house. They heard him grab his bicycle and then the gate slammed.

'If you're not careful, you'll lose him,' Janey said quietly. 'He'll do what he wants without your permission.'

For what seemed a long time they stood in silence. Then Ashe began to walk towards the house.

'I won't stay for a meal, thank you,' he said. 'I think I should go home.'

Ashe's Blessing

For the next few days, Janey threw herself into her work at Forge Antiques, not allowing herself to think of Ashe. She and Martin took a trip into Wales to attend a large antiques fair. Martin was looking for enamelled boxes as usual while Janey took the opportunity to build up her collection of jewellery. She found people friendly and helpful and made several useful contacts.

Martin smiled approvingly when he saw her talking to experts and stall holders. This was obviously what he'd hoped Amelie would be doing.

On the way home, they stopped for a meal. When they'd eaten, Martin sat back in his chair and looked at his cousin.

'I've made a decision,' he said, 'about your future.'

She regarded him warily. She hadn't

told Martin or Amelie about her disagreement with Ashe. It hurt too much for discussion.

'I want to make you a partner in the business,' Martin said.

A partner! This was a surprise. Martin was very possessive of his business and Janey had never dreamed he'd want anyone else to make decisions about it.

'But partners put money into businesses,' she said. 'I can't do that, as you know.'

'I don't want you to contribute financially, I just want your wholehearted support.'

'You know you have that anyway.'

'But this would put it on a legal footing,' he said. 'You've been so loyal, so helpful to me and to Amelie, I want you to know how much I appreciate it.'

'I don't know what to say.' Janey looked into the distance. What about her writing? Would being a partner mean that she had less time for that?

'I can't give you more of my time,' she said at last. 'I'm flattered that you should suggest it, but I must have time for my own interests.'

He smiled.

'I know what you're thinking. Don't worry. I shan't expect you to spend any more time at Forge Antiques than you do now.' He stirred his coffee. 'So what do you say?'

'Thank you. I shall be pleased and proud to be a director of Forge Antiques.'

'Let's drink to that,' Martin said, raising his coffee cup.

* * *

An excited Ceri called at the cottage the next evening.

'Guess what!' she burst out before even removing her coat. 'Wynn is testing me for his next film.'

'He was obviously impressed by your performance in this one,' Janey said. 'Is it the lead?'

'No. Second lead. But it's quite a big part.'

'Is it a costume film again?'

'No, modern. He's already cast the men. You should see the one who's opposite me. He's Greek. His name is John.' Ceri had a dreamy look in her eyes.

'Is he better than Kyle?'

'Completely different.' Ceri flicked her fingers in the air. 'Kyle was a mere boy. John is a man.' She gave Janey a wicked smile. 'And how's your love life? Where's the desirable Ashe Corby?'

For answer, Janey burst into tears.

Ceri flung herself on her knees beside her friend and put her arms round her.

'Whatever's wrong, Janey? Is it finished?'

Janey sobbed for a few minutes then sat up, fumbled for a tissue and wiped her eyes.

'I didn't want to talk about it, but it might help.' Slowly she told Ceri all about Daniel, the garden and the competition.

'And he's absolutely against Daniel taking up horticulture? The boy can't persuade him?'

'He wants Daniel to go into the firm.

He won't even discuss it.'

'And he blames you for encouraging Daniel?'

Janey nodded.

'He's right. I interfered. But I'm very fond of Daniel. He's a lovely boy and apart from the housekeeper who brought him up, and his cousin Imogen, he has nobody on his side. His mother is dead and his father seems unable to communicate with him.'

'Perhaps he finds being mother and father too difficult,' Ceri said. 'He wants to do what's best for Daniel and the family firm. What are you going to do?'

'I don't know. I've been waiting to see what happens, but he hasn't been in touch. I haven't seen Daniel either. Probably Ashe has told him not to see me.' Tears began to fall again.

Ceri returned to her chair.

'I think that when the situation is very difficult, it's best to do nothing,' she said. 'Just wait and see how it resolves itself. Now dry your eyes. I'm going to make us some of my special scrambled eggs on toast and then we're going to play Scrabble. Take your mind off your troubles.'

Janey gave her eyes a final wipe and smiled at her friend.

'What a good idea. Just what I feel like.'

The next day, Kevin, in a very expensive new suede jacket, pushed open the door of the shop. Janey was alone. Amelie was at the nursery and Martin had gone over to see Reg Driver, the valuer.

'You know why I've come.'

Janey made no reply.

'You promised to think about my proposal. Well?'

'I've thought, and I'm afraid my answer is still no.'

Kevin breathed heavily.

'Very well, I shan't ask again. But I'm sorry, very sorry, and I think you will be, too, in time. You won't get a better offer. Goodbye, Janey.'

He swung round and left the shop slamming the door behind him.

Janey breathed a sigh of relief. After all this time, she was rid of him at last.

Ten minutes later, she was pleased to see Daniel enter the shop. He looked a little shamefaced.

'I'm sorry I haven't come to see you,' he said, 'but my father . . . '

'He told you not to see me,' Janey guessed.

'He's very angry. Maybe we should have told him earlier on. But then he'd have stopped me entering the competition.' He put a hand on Janey's arm. 'I'm sorry you and he . . . you know. I think you were right for him.'

Janey bit her lip.

'Perhaps we weren't right together.' But she knew she didn't believe it.

'How is he?'

'Miserable,' he said. 'Miserable and sad. I think he misses you. Carli thinks so, too. I wish I could bring you together again.'

Janey straightened her shoulders and took a deep breath.

'And what about you? Any news?'

He looked at her with an expression-less face, took a letter from his pocket and laid it on the counter.

They looked at each other and he pushed the envelope towards her. Slowly she opened it and read the contents.

'Wow! You've done it. You've won!'

They flung their arms around each other and hugged, thoughts of Ashe's antagonism forgotten.

'When did you hear?'

'This morning. I had to come and tell you, whatever my father said.'

'I can't believe it! Well, of course, I knew you'd win,' she said loyally, 'but I just can't believe it now it's happened. We must have a toast.' She rushed into the office and came out with a bottle and two glasses.

Daniel examined the bottle.

'Non-alchoholic wine?'

'I can't have your father blamimg me for encouraging you to drink,' she said. 'This is very nice.'

They toasted Daniel's success and his future. Then they toasted Janey's promotion to partner.

When Martin came in they were decidedly merry on non-alchoholic wine.

'What happens now?' Martin asked when the reason for the celebration had been explained to him.

'I shall have to go to the college for interviews. It won't cost my father anything, the magazine will sponsor me. But no doubt there will be problems.'

She could see he didn't want to discuss the trouble with Martin. Martin disappeared into the office after congratulating Daniel again.

'My aunt, Imogen's mum, has offered Dad all her shares in the firm if he'll take Imogen into the business,' Daniel said. 'He won't. He doesn't want a woman eventually leading the company. He wants me,' he said bitterly.

'Does he know you've won the competition?'

'I told him. He said congratulations. He said he wasn't surprised, the garden was beautiful.'

'Well, that's something.'

'He still won't discuss the future.' Daniel replaced the letter in his pocket. 'So we wait until something happens.'

Janey thought of Ceri's advice. Perhaps it was the right thing for all of them.

She telephoned Jim that evening.

'I don't think I'll have any more archery lessons,' she said.

'Why not? You're doing so well.'

Janey was silent.

'Has something happened between you and Ashe?' he asked. 'He's like a bear with a sore head at the moment. We all have to watch what we say. Are you the cause of it?'

'You could say that. He says I've interfered between him and Daniel. I haven't seen him for a while. Perhaps I won't see him again.'

'Difficult,' Jim said, obviously not wanting to become involved.

Janey thanked him again for the lessons, said how she'd enjoyed them and rang off. There was nothing more to say. Ashe wouldn't be interested now.

A few days later, Martin came into

the shop with the air of someone bringing extraordinary news.

'Guess what I've heard,' he said. 'Kevin has left for Scotland and who do you think has gone with him?'

'How should I know?' Janey was just glad that it wasn't her.

'Carole.'

'Carole? Do I know her?'

'Do you remember at the club dance? Carole, the platinum blonde?'

Janey remembered. Carole — the reason Martin had been missing when the telephone call came.

'Kevin brought her to the dance. Now they've gone to Scotland together. They're to be married.'

'I hope they'll be very happy,' Janey said automatically.

Privately she thought they deserved one another.

A week later, Daniel called at the cottage. Pixie, who hadn't seen him for a while, gave him a joyful welcome and presented all her toys.

'Wait a minute,' he said. 'I'll play with

you later. I want to talk to Janey.'

'The most amazing thing,' he told her. 'I'm pleased but I'm also scared. I don't know if I can do it.'

'What? What's happened? Tell me.'

'I've agreed to be interviewed on television in a gardening programme.'

'Daniel! When?'

'On Wednesday week. Mr Dukes, my form master, has said he'll go with me.'

'Does your father know?'

'I haven't mentioned it. He'll take great delight in not watching if I do. Carli knows. She's thrilled but she won't tell Dad.'

'You should tell him. I'm sure he'd be pleased,' Janey said, feeling that Ashe was being portrayed as an ogre.

Daniel didn't comment.

'I hope you don't mind,' he said, 'but the television people are phoning you tomorrow about filming the garden.'

'I couldn't . . . ' Janey began.

'You don't need to be here. Or you can stay in the house and watch from the window. I'll see to everything.'

'Goodness, things are moving fast. Have you heard from the college?'

'No. It's early days.'

Pixie squealed and Daniel relented.

'Come on, then.' He took the little dog into the garden.

Janey watched them from the window. Poor Daniel. Things were going right and wrong for him.

For her, as far as her love life was concerned, things were only going wrong.

On the day of the television broadcast, Janey came to a decision. She picked up the telephone and dialled Ashe's number.

'Ashe, it's Janey,' she said as soon as he answered and before she could lose her courage.

'Janey, how are you?' He didn't exactly sound friendly but at least he was prepared to talk to her.

'I want to ask you a favour. Will you come over here at seven o'clock? I want to show you something.'

'Seven o'clock. That's dinnertime.'

Janey waited. Should she offer to cook him a meal? No, that was a step too far. So she waited.

'I suppose I could have something earlier. Is it important?'

'Very important.'

He sighed.

'Very well. I'll see you at seven.'

At seven o'clock promptly, Ashe rang the bell. Their greetings were cool but not unfriendly. Janey sat him on the couch opposite the television, poured two glasses of wine and placed a tray of nuts on the little table between them. Ashe looked surprised but said nothing.

She switched on the television and sat on the couch, but at the furthest end from him.

The gardening programme began. Ashe shot her a quick glance but she stared straight ahead. She felt a tingling in her spine. Does he know why he's here, she wondered. Surely he must know. But if he did, he was concealing it very well.

They sat through a discussion on growing roses then the camera focused on the presenter.

'We have an unusual item this evening,' he began. 'As I'm sure you all know, one magazine has been running a competition to find a future garden designer. The winner is here with us in the studio, a young man, only sixteen and still at school. Daniel Corby.'

A very nervous-looking Daniel came into the studio to a round of applause. The interview lasted only for about six minutes, but to Janey it seemed to go on for ever. She daren't look at Ashe who sat motionless at his end of the couch.

Daniel was asked about his future plans and said that he was excited to be going to college to study horticulture. Enlarged pictures of Janey's garden, before and after Daniel's treatment, were shown and earned another round of applause.

Janey risked a quick glance at Ashe. His face was impassive. He didn't look at her.

When the programme ended, Ashe helped himself to some nuts and accepted Janey's invitation to another glass of wine. It was as though he was there for a normal social evening.

Then to Janey's amazement, he began to talk about Imogen.

'I think I told you before how impressed I was by her general intelligence,' he said. 'She'd be an asset to any company, so I've decided to take her into the family firm.'

I haven't asked you here to talk about Imogen, Janey thought, exasperated.

'And Daniel?'

'You heard him. He's going to horticultural college.'

'With your blessing?'

Ashe hesitated.

'After that programme, even I have to admit that he would be wasting his talents if he didn't take up horticulture. Yes, with my blessing.'

Without thinking, Janey flung herself ito his arms and hugged him.

'Thank you,' she said emotionally. 'Thank you.'

Then realising what she was doing, she flushed and moved away from him.

'I'm sorry. I don't know what came over me.'

'I think your affection for my son came over you. When Daniel's mother died, I was devastated,' he said quietly. 'I couldn't come to terms with being everything to this little boy. And there was the business . . . ' His voice tailed off. 'I left his rearing to Mrs Carlson. She's been wonderful. She and Daniel adore each other. But I was wrong not to play a larger part in Daniel's life. I hope I can change that now.'

He reached out and took her in his arms.

'You've been an inspiration to Daniel. We had a long talk about everything you've done for him. I can never thank you enough for the care you've given him.'

He looked down into her eyes.

'I've missed you so much, Janey. I reacted without taking anyone else's point of view into consideration. When I was young, I had dreams. Daniel was entitled to his dreams. I'm so sorry. Can you forgive me?'

Janey couldn't speak but the fervour with which she returned his kisses told him all he needed to know.

'One thing puzzles me,' she said, sitting up. 'If you and Daniel had a long talk, and if you decided that I had helped him, why didn't you contact me?'

'I didn't think you'd want to speak to me again,' he said simply.

She turned to look at him.

'If you knew just how I'd missed you.'

'Janey, we've wasted more than three weeks of our lives. Let's forget this ever happened. Let's start again.'

She nodded, not trusting herself to speak.

'Now, tell me all you've been doing,' he said, settling her head comfortably against his shoulder.

So she told him about her trip to Wales and her promotion to partner in the company.

He was suitably impressed.

'As long as it leaves time for your writing,' he said.

She reached up and kissed him.

'Thank you.'

'For what?'

'For taking my writing seriously. Not everyone does.' For a second she thought of Kevin and his snide remarks. Hastily she pushed him out of her mind.

Her little chiming clock reminded them that it was getting late. Reluctantly, he stood up.

'I really must be getting back. I have an early start in the morning.'

She walked with him to the door.

'Dinner tomorrow night?' he asked.

'That would be lovely.'

One more kiss and he was gone. Janey leaned back against the door, a dreamy look on her face.

Darling Ashe. Everything was as it had been — but better. Daniel and Imogen would realise their ambitions and she and Ashe would fall deeper in love and then — who knows?

A soft knock on the door startled her and she jumped away from it. Who could it be at this time of night.

'Janey,' a hushed voice called, 'open the door. I've just realised something important.'

Quickly she unlocked it and flung it open.

Ashe strode in with a serious look on his face.

'Something important?' she queried.

'Yes. We've settled Daniel and Imogen's futures. What about ours?' He smiled and took her hands. 'Janey, will you marry me?'

She melted into his arms.

'Yes, Ashe, of course I will.'

Words were unnecessary for several moments.

'It will have to be soon. I leave for America in a month.'

She looked dismayed.

'America. The film! I'd forgotten.'

He smiled.

'But you'll come, too. It will be our honeymoon. What do you say?'

Her sparkling eyes gave him her answer.

'I think it's a fairytale ending,' she said.

THE END

We do hope that you have enjoyed reading this large print book.

Did you know that all of our titles are available for purchase?

We publish a wide range of high quality large print books including:
Romances, Mysteries, Classics
General Fiction
Non Fiction and Westerns

Special interest titles available in large print are:
The Little Oxford Dictionary
Music Book, Song Book
Hymn Book, Service Book

Also available from us courtesy of Oxford University Press:
Young Readers' Dictionary
(large print edition)
Young Readers' Thesaurus
(large print edition)

For further information or a free brochure, please contact us at:
Ulverscroft Large Print Books Ltd.,
The Green, Bradgate Road, Anstey,
Leicester, LE7 7FU, England.
Tel: (00 44) **0116 236 4325**
Fax: (00 44) **0116 234 0205**

Other titles in the
Linford Romance Library:

HUSHED WORDS

Angela Britnell

Cassie, a struggling single mother, and Jay, a wealthy financier, share a holiday romance in Italy; when fate throws them together again their sizzling passion rekindles. Cassie's family problems combined with Jay's fear of commitment and growing dissatisfaction with his lifestyle make their idea of a future together a dream. Jay can't ask for a second chance with Cassie until he discovers a new direction in life and lays it all on the line with the woman he loves.